THE KEY OF

CHARMAIN ZIMMERMAN BRACKETT

DIAMOND KEY PRESS

Published June 2012, July 2015

Second Edition

ISBN-10:
0985625902
ISBN-13:
978-0-9856259-0-0

This book is dedicated to my husband, Bret, who believes in my crazy dreams.

Special thanks to Leonard "Porkchop" Zimmerman Jr., Bill and Bea Baab, Melanie Nowlin, Ashlee Henry for your input. I could not have done this without you.

Thanks also to my children, Jessica, Jeremy and Allie and my parents, Nona and Leonard Zimmerman Sr., for their encouragement.

THE KEY OF ELYON

THE KEY OF ELYON

1

Stephen jolted out of a deep sleep and sat up in his bed gasping for breath. The hairs on the back of his neck stood on edge as a tingle shot down his spine. He glanced around the room. Everything seemed fine. Nothing was out of place. The moonlight flooded the room. He could hear the winter wind howling, and a tree branch gently tapping on the panes.

No. That wasn't it, the 12 year-old thought. He remained motionless in his bed, straining his ear to hear the faint sound. *Was it all a dream? Or was it something else?*

"Stephen," a soft voice called to him.

The only other person in their home was his grandfather, John. Stephen was afraid. Something must be wrong. He scampered out of bed and headed toward his grandfather's room.

"Papa, I'm here," Stephen said, opening the door and rushing to his grandfather's bedside.

His grandfather turned, and in a muffled voice, he asked what Stephen wanted.

"You called me," Stephen replied.

Papa rolled back over.

"No, I didn't call you. Go back to sleep," he said.

Stephen was sure he'd heard something. It seemed so real, but maybe it was just a dream after all. Maybe it was the wind; maybe it was nothing at all. He walked out into the hallway. It was dark and drafty in the old house. It made unusual noises sometimes. He looked around. He shrugged it off as he climbed into bed and tried to go back to sleep.

Just as he fell into a slumber, he heard the voice again.

"Stephen," the voice called.

He only heard his name. He had never known of his grandfather to talk in his sleep. Sleepier this time, Stephen dragged himself out of his bed and headed to his grandfather's room. He stood at the door and listened for a moment. No, his grandfather wasn't talking in his sleep.

"Papa, did you call me?" Stephen asked as he rubbed his eyes.

"No, I didn't," his grandfather replied.

Stephen headed back to his room, confused by the voice he was hearing.

His grandfather, John, was now awake. He knew the source of the voice. He'd known it in his younger days, but as time had passed, he'd walked away. He felt a stab of pain. His heart longed to revisit those days.

Was it too late? John wondered. *What was happening?*

Stephen tried to go back to sleep, but now he was curious and awake. He wondered about the voice calling out to him. His mind began to wander. There were other mysteries in the house especially the locked room at the end of the hallway. He'd only seen inside it through a keyhole. Despite the fact that it was kept locked, there was always light streaming from its crevices.

Why would lights always be on in an unused, locked room? he pondered.

He sat in his bed with his legs crossed. He rested his chin in his hands and leaned his elbows on his knees. He loved his Papa, but Stephen often imagined what could be behind those doors. He wondered why John kept secrets. It wasn't long before Stephen leaned back into his pillows and drifted back to sleep.

But the sleep was short-lived as the January wind ripped through the open window, blowing the curtains wildly and rushing across

Stephen's body. He awoke and shivered.

"How did the window open?" he thought. He was sure his grandfather had checked the lock before they went to sleep.

Stephen jumped out of the bed to close and lock the window. Once again, he heard the voice. It seemed louder now. It wasn't a dream, and he wasn't imagining things. Since it wasn't his grandfather the past two times, Stephen decided to investigate. He stood still until he heard the voice again.

"Stephen."

It seemed louder than a whisper, but he didn't know which direction it was coming from.

"Yes, I'm here," he replied. He felt silly doing it. He knew no one was there.

He walked out of his room and listened once more.

"Stephen."

The voice seemed to be coming from the secret room. Stephen's heart began to beat faster as the voice became louder and louder. He was going to get in a lot of trouble if his grandfather found out. He tried not to be afraid. He was torn between finding out the source of the voice and wondering how he might be punished. Would he lose his phone or video games? He hesitated, but the voice continued to call him. He couldn't think about the punishment. He had to know who or what was calling to him. He tried to tiptoe down the hallway, but he found himself running toward the closed door. Even though he was running as fast as he could, he felt as though weights were tied to his feet. The voice was irresistible to him, drawing him closer. He had to get into that room.

He stopped at the oak door and paused. Light seeped underneath it and around its edges. He bent down to look into the keyhole, but he couldn't see anything except light.

He placed his hand on the brass doorknob and paused. Timidly, he turned the knob, not expecting it to open. He was surprised it wasn't locked. He'd never been able to open it before, and he'd tried many times. He slowly pushed open the large oak door, its hinges squeaking. The room was filled with bookcases which climbed toward the towering ceiling. Stephen's attention was not on the hundreds of books in the room, but the one in its center. On a golden table was the biggest book he'd never seen. It must've measured at least four feet in width. And it was open.

What was most curious about the book wasn't its size, but the fact that it was illuminated. There were no lights shining down on it; however, rays of light seemed to be coming from the book itself. As he gazed on the book, Stephen felt it drawing him toward it. Then he heard that voice again.

"Stephen. Stephen," it called to him.

Stephen shuffled toward the book. He was mesmerized. His eyes grew wide, and his mouth dropped as he gazed on the intense light shooting from it. He peered underneath the book and walked in a circle around it. He'd never seen anything like it.

John had heard Stephen's footsteps down the hallway so he got up to follow his grandson. He kept his distance not wanting to break into the moment. He could see into the room through the door Stephen had left open. John had hoped for this day to come and felt his heart burn. He knew the great adventure Stephen was about to embark on and felt the crushing weight of the years of bitterness that had closed off his heart. He longed to go with Stephen, and somehow, he knew if he could let go of the past, he could be right there with him. Letting go had been so hard for him.

He tried to push back the memories of the pain that caused him to walk away from such a special relationship he'd had. Tears began to fall as he watched Stephen approach the book.

Stephen wasn't quite tall enough to view the pages so he looked around for something to stand on. He saw a footrest nearby and pulled it in front of the book. He stepped onto it and strained his neck to view the large pages. But the light was too bright. He was torn between shielding his eyes and letting his curiosity get the better of him. He lost his balance on the stool and tumbled into the book. He knew he'd fallen into the book, but he felt like he was flying instead, traveling upward through this amazing corridor of light mixed with the most beautiful colors he'd ever seen. The passageway had brilliant blues, purples, reds, and greens. These weren't pale pastels, but the colors of rich, polished gems. There were other hues he'd never seen and couldn't describe. Each one wrapped around him as he hurtled through the portal. He was amazed as all the fear he'd felt vanished. He wasn't worried that he'd gone into the forbidden room or what his grandfather would say or do. None of that seemed to matter. He had never sensed such peace.

Stephen's grandfather watched it all and slowly followed into the room. He walked over to the book. While the rays of light were blinding to Stephen, they were only dim glimmers to his grandfather. His bitterness and sadness blocked them from his view. He gently touched the pages; the sadness seemed more than he could bear.

"John," he faintly heard the voice call his name.

Stephen couldn't tell how much time had passed as he glided through the portal. Then, all of a sudden, he stopped. He looked around. The bright light he had seen from the book seemed to envelop the whole place he was in now. There was no darkness at all. He looked around, trying to figure out where he was.

He seemed to be inside a palace of some kind, but it was nothing like any he'd ever seen in movies or imagined. The room was massive, and everything seemed to be made of precious jewels rather than granite, wood or metal. The floors and walls were made from iridescent pearls. Single gems fashioned the 20-foot tall columns. There were rubies, sapphires and emeralds. The light pierced through them and filled the room with vibrant colors.

As he stood in awe of the breathtaking colors, he began to notice there were many different types of beings in this place. Stephen couldn't call them people because they weren't human. One type of these creatures had massive wings and four different faces including that of a man and a bird. There were other creatures, and they were made in the shape of circles. These circles had circles inside them, and they had many eyes. They whisked throughout the air without turning their bodies, and they glided upon the floor. Stephen couldn't help but stare at them. The creatures glanced at him, but they were silent. Their attention was fixed elsewhere in the room.

Another creature had the head and wings of an eagle, but it had hands and legs like a man. It could fly, but it could also walk. There were many women there as well. They were dressed in long dresses similar to those women might have worn during the Medieval times. Their dresses were made of velvety material of rich reds, purples, and blues, and they were embroidered in gold. Their long sleeves flowed. All of them wore their hair in braids. Some of them had very long hair intertwined with ribbons of gold. As they turned, he noticed they had wings as well. Many of them seemed to be singing softly. There was a beautiful sound radiating through the place.

Also, there were creatures made of flames. These were Stephen's favorites. They flew around the room somehow. They didn't have wings but were just bursts of colors - red, orange, yellow. They didn't have distinct features except for their eyes which sparkled like diamonds in the midst of the flames. Despite their wild appearance, Stephen wasn't afraid of them. He sensed they wouldn't hurt him.

As Stephen was taking in everything around him, he heard voices, and immediately, he recognized one of them as the voice which had called out to him.

"We have people scattered around, but they aren't unified. The battles have taken their toll on them. I need someone to go for me. I need a champion to rally the people together. They need hope, and they must be ready," the voice said. "The time is drawing near."

Stephen moved closer to see the source of the voice. Stephen could see who he was talking to. They were two tall and muscular manlike creatures. They wore the clothing of ancient soldiers with helmets and armor. Their swords were taller than Stephen. Their blades seemed to be some type of glowing metal. Stephen squinted. No, that wasn't metal at all. Their blades were of the same light which illuminated this place he was in.

"Yes, my lord, this is true. They've waited a long time for your return. Many of them doubt you will be coming back. They've lost sight of the things you've told them. They are tired," said one of the soldiers.

Stephen tried to get closer to see the faces of these soldiers and to get a look at the one who must be the ruler here – the one who had called him by name. This king was seated on a throne of light. He had a youthful appearance. He was muscular, and even though he was seated, Stephen could tell he was tall. He had the face of a man. He had bronze-colored skin, and his long hair shimmered like gold. His entire body seemed to glow. As Stephen looked at him, he had a passing thought that all of the light in the entire place seemed to come from this one being. That made no sense to Stephen, but at the same time, it did.

"There are still things that must be accomplished before I come, however. It is not yet time. Things that were foretold must come to pass," the king said. "It won't be long before all the things that are meant to be will be."

Stephen wondered what this was all about. He began to get nervous as he eavesdropped.

Was I the champion this king needed? Was I important enough that a king from another world would call to me? Why would a king want me?

Stephen wanted to run and hide or maybe just to go home. He didn't understand what was going on. He was only 12.

He soon discovered that his bare feet weren't listening to his head. He rushed to the king. He knew from the movies he'd seen that he should bow or kneel in front of him.

"I will go. I am the one. Please let me do it," Stephen said.

As he bowed, he saw his clothes. He'd forgotten that he was wearing his superhero pajamas. He clamped his hands over his mouth, but it was too late. The words had escaped before he had a chance to stop them. Immediately, the king stopped speaking and looked at Stephen, who was kneeling before him. He kept his head bowed. He couldn't believe what he had just done. He had just volunteered to help a king who had soldiers much bigger and stronger than Stephen was. A multitude of thoughts ran quickly through his head.

Stephen felt a hand on his shoulder as he kept his eyes fixed on the feet of the king. Although the king was wearing a long robe, Stephen could see his sandaled feet. He didn't feel so bad about his own bare feet. He slowly looked up into the face of this king, and their eyes met. As they glanced at each other, all of Stephen's thoughts of inadequacy ceased. The king's eyes were the brightest blue he'd ever seen, and instead of feeling stupid for what he'd done, Stephen felt accepted. It didn't matter that he was a child. The more Stephen looked at this being, the more he felt like he knew this king. Stephen looked at his face and saw his beautiful eyes, and Stephen felt comfortable in the king's presence.

The king smiled.

"I know you will," he said. "I have called many, but they have not responded to me. They thought my voice was the wind or their imagination. Or they let the day-to-day cares stop them from answering."

Stephen wondered if he was speaking of his grandfather. After all, he did come through the book inside Papa's house. What did Papa know?

"There's much preparation to be done, my young one," said the king. "You have much to learn, but you will learn quickly. There isn't much time."

He motioned for Stephen to stand.

"Welcome, Stephen. I am Elyon," he said as he turned to look at one of the fire creatures. He nodded, and the fiery one flew through the air to a golden cabinet. It took a scroll from out of the cabinet and brought it to the king. Stephen's mouth fell open as he watched the fire creature hold the scroll. Elyon took the scroll, and it hadn't caught on fire even though it was surrounded by flames.

"Stephen, you must learn my words, and you must learn my ways," said Elyon. Stephen watched as Elyon took the scroll and flicked his wrist. Stephen couldn't believe his eyes as he watched the scroll shrink into a bite-sized piece.

"Take and eat this, my son," said Elyon.

Stephen took it from the king's hand and stared at it for a minute. He didn't think it would hurt him. It melted in his mouth and tasted sweet like honey.

"My words must become part of you. My words are written in the book that brought you here to me. You will live and breathe my words. They will strengthen you in times of weakness; they will give you hope when you are discouraged; and they will provide you wisdom when don't know what to do," he said. "I know you don't understand, but you will in time. You will be my ambassador, my emissary in your world."

Stephen was trying to take in everything; there was so much he had questions about.

"I have something else for you," Elyon said.

Stephen stretched out his hand. Elyon placed a golden key in Stephen's palm and closed his hand around it. His head was spinning. He didn't even know why he was drawn to help this king. He didn't know anything about him or this quest. What would he even be doing?

"Much of what you need to know is found within the Book of Ancient Wisdom, which is in your grandfather's house," said Elyon. "He has been one of my caretakers for many years. It contains principles which you must follow if you are to successfully lead. I realize that you have many questions. Things will not always make sense to you, and you can never rely completely on your senses. They will lie to you."

The king turned and motioned to a man standing next to him. Stephen hadn't seen him until then. Where did he come from? He didn't look like anyone else in the room. He was about seven feet tall and muscular. He had dark black shoulder-length wavy hair and was wearing a full-length black leather duster coat, black pants and a black shirt. He was out of place when compared to the rest of those in Elyon's world. Even though he was in all black, his face was bright , and his eyes sparkled as he smiled at Stephen.

"This is Belshazzon," said the king. "He has taken this form and is dressed this way because this is the image you have of someone who could protect you. That's his job. He will be your guard and help you in your journey. It will not be an easy one, but you will never be left alone. Belshazzon has special abilities, which you will learn in time. You will not always be able to see him nor will those around you. But you must know he is there."

Belshazzon smiled and nodded at Stephen.

2

John thought about what Stephen must be experiencing. He'd heard so many stories. He knew it would be exciting for Stephen, but at the same time, he was sad. He sat down on the floor next to the book and sobbed. He'd known a little about the Book of Ancient Wisdom and had seen many marvelous things as a young man. He didn't travel to the world that Stephen traveled to but met Elyon in a different way. Elyon communicated to John through his mind, his thoughts, his dreams. He received many ideas from his association with Elyon, and at a young age, he used them to invent many things which made him rich.

His inventions were a distraction to him from his ultimate purpose. He had started his training, but then he met a young woman, Meredith. She had a wild streak, but John couldn't resist her. From the beginning, he knew that she would probably break his heart and that he should stay away from her. She wasn't the type of woman to settle down and have a family. She longed for too much adventure of the wrong kind, and she had had run-ins with the law usually after nights of wild parties. Those only seemed to fuel her desire to go after the wrong things and the wrong people.

Underneath, Meredith just wanted someone to love her, but because of an abusive relationship with her father, she couldn't accept the love John had for her. John practically worshipped the ground she walked on; there was nothing he wouldn't have done for her.

Meredith agreed to marry him, but true to her past, she sabotaged anything good that came to her. Within a year, their son, Aaron, was born, and Meredith was gone. The fairytale had come true, but Meredith couldn't be the fairytale princess. It broke John's heart that she left, and he vowed he'd never let anyone that close to him ever again. He felt like he'd been the fool, and he'd allowed her to play with his heart and his life. He put up many walls. Within five years of Meredith's departure, both of John's parents died. He locked himself away in the home that had been in his family for several generations.

He devoted himself to Aaron and forgot the Book of Ancient Wisdom. His heart became bitter as he blamed Elyon for the pain he felt. Elyon could have done something to stop Meredith from leaving, or he could have brought her back, so John thought. But Elyon didn't do what John wanted him to so John didn't teach Aaron the ways he knew.

Aaron had a lot of his mother's untamed spirit in him. When Aaron was18, he left his father's house after a fight. He vowed to never return, and he never did.

John tried to return to his ideas and finish the inventions he had started, but nothing mattered. He closed the door to the room housing the Book of Ancient Wisdom, and he locked it away.

Then, about four years after Aaron had left in his anger, a woman arrived at John's door. She explained she represented the state. His son, Aaron, and his daughter-in-law, Melissa, had been killed in a car crash. They had an infant son, Stephen, who had been with a babysitter during the crash. Melissa had no family, and John was the only known member of Aaron's family. John took the baby in and hoped for a second chance. He didn't feel he'd been the kind of parent he should have, but this time, he vowed to do things differently. He wanted to be a better father.

There were many times that John passed the room containing the book. He would pause by the door, but he never went in. He figured that he'd strayed too far to ever go back to the path he always knew he should follow.

As he sat on the floor, John realized his task would fall upon his grandson who was now with Elyon. He wondered what it was like. The stories his father and grandfather told him about the king began to flood his mind. He remembered thinking they were just too marvelous, too good to be true, but his family believed them. He could see the night his grandfather told him about the boy who was foretold and would lead Elyon's people. Why was all of this flooding back as if it only happened yesterday? Could Stephen be the one?

He knew he had another chance to make a difference.

"John."

The voice cut through his daydreams, and this time, it was louder than before.

"Elyon," he replied through the tears.

A ray of hope broke through years of bitterness and pain. He began to think maybe he was wrong about some things. If Elyon had not forced John to follow the path he was destined for, why would Elyon force anyone else to do something? People make their own choices, and sometimes those choices hurt the ones they love. The dull ache remained, but he could feel some of the sadness leave. John knew that he would do what he needed to do. He knew of the battle that was to come, and Stephen had the blood of the ancients running through him. There was something in his DNA, which shaped him for this moment in time. John knew Stephen was destined to be the one Elyon would use, but could he help him in his mission?

While this evening was exciting for both Stephen and John, not everyone was happy about what was taking place with them. An ominous figure approached the door. Even hunched over, the creature was about six feet tall with bat-like wings which when opened to full width, would span six feet. Hairless, his skin was ashen, and he had large eyes and gnarled fangs. Instead of a nose, he had two short curved tusks. His bony arms were fashioned with sharp claws on the ends of his bony hands. The bottom half of his body resembled a bird of prey with razor-sharp talons. He was repulsive and fierce-looking.

As he stood at the door staring at John's weeping figure, several other creatures identical to him arrived at his side. His name was Lemachor, a captain of an Army of the dark lord, Gravinder. His job had been to thwart Elyon's plan in this family and ultimately to Elyon's many subjects in this realm. He'd been successful in keeping them neutralized for many years. They focused more on their own lives and the lives of family members rather than their mission.

This was a bad sign; no one had ventured into the book in decades. Stephen's grandfather had gotten close and did hear Elyon's call, but they were able to stop him from doing any real damage to Gravinder's plan. These humans were easy to control and manipulate through their emotions.

Lemachor knew of the ancient prophecies, however. He knew they could only delay them from coming to pass. Lemachor turned to his soldiers.

"We are losing ground on this night," Lemachor told them. "For generations, we have kept this family from its mission The boy is with Elyon now, and this could tip the scales in the favor of his family and of Elyon's subjects. The time foretold may be at hand. Ready yourselves for a fight."

Lemachor and the others couldn't enter the room with the book. To touch it or even hear its content tormented them. They weren't just words, but there was a life force behind them. Lemachor and his band had to keep the boy and his grandfather from getting to the book and learning its secrets - and theirs.

Stephen heard the grandfather clock in the living room chime. He opened his eyes to look around. He was confused. He wondered how he got back and if it had been just a dream. He sat up and looked around his room. That wonderful place seemed real enough, but he wasn't sure until he saw something out of the corner of his eye. He turned and looked on his pillow, where he saw the key Elyon had given him. Moonbeams bounced off of it. He reached out and gently ran a finger across the cold metal.

It was real.

Stephen grabbed the key and excitedly ran down the hall to find his grandfather. He had to tell him. He ran past Lemachor and his warriors. As he did, he felt the hairs on the back of his neck stand on edge. It was as though he'd run through an arctic blast. He shivered, but he couldn't stop to figure it out. Lemachor stared at his warriors. They noticed as Stephen shivered. He was becoming aware and that wasn't good for them.

Stephen ran down the hallway and noticed the clock. It was 2 a.m. He saw his grandfather in the room, sitting on the floor by the golden table. He was slumped over; he had fallen asleep there.

"Papa," said Stephen as he knelt and grabbed his grandfather's shoulder, shaking him. "It was real. I knew it was real."

Stephen's mind started racing. Where to start? What questions to ask? He didn't even know. He knew it was the middle of the night, but he didn't want to go back to sleep.

His grandfather glanced at Stephen and smiled.

"It's real, Papa," he said. "It was all real."

Papa nodded.

"Yes, Stephen. It's more real than this room you and I are in. It's more real than you'll ever know."

He stood up and looked at Stephen.

"We have a lot to talk about in the morning," John said

"Can't we talk about it now?" Stephen asked.

"In the morning, Stephen. You and I have some catching up to do, but first, let's get some sleep."

John headed toward the door where he paused. Stephen had lingered. He stood near the center of the room and slowly turned in a circle. He wanted to take in every inch of the room. The Book of Ancient Wisdom was in the center. The windows were covered with heavy drapes, which kept the sun and moonlight out. It didn't matter because the room was filled with the light exuding from the book.

Stephen walked over to it and touched its pages remembering how through it, he went to the most beautiful place. Stephen stared at the pages. He looked at the words. At first, he couldn't understand them. They were in an ancient language, but then he remembered the scroll Elyon had fed him. He thought that was strange at the time. As he stared at the pages, the letters floated off the page and translated into modern day English so he could easily read them.

"Your battles are not against other people but against the dark forces from other realms."

What a cryptic message, he thought.

He felt a hand on his shoulder and turned to see his grandfather.

"This will be here in the morning. Time to go back to bed," he said.

Stephen followed his grandfather's lead, turning to leave the room, but he didn't want to go. He wanted to learn the mysteries. He paused at the door, wondering whether to close it or not. He left it open and headed down the hallway.

Lemachor and some of his best soldiers stood at the door.

As Stephen passed them, he once again felt extreme cold. He looked around in the darkness, and he thought he saw something. He blinked as his and Lemachor's eyes briefly locked. Stephen wasn't sure of what he was seeing. He blinked, and whatever it was - was gone. Stephen shook his head. He wondered if he was more tired than he realized. Lemachor had vanished around the corner. Up until that point, his greatest weapon had been the fact that he and the others could move around the house undetected, but Stephen had gone into Elyon's realm. His eyes were now opened to the other world.

Lemachor had to regroup. A key to his new plan would be keeping Stephen and his grandfather out of the room and away from that book. He couldn't allow either of them to go into that realm again. Lemachor just had to convince Stephen he didn't see anything at all. That is was just a dream or his imagination. After all, it had been a long night; surely, he was just seeing things.

"Block the door! Do not allow them back into this room!" Lemachor roared. Immediately, two Lemachor clones appeared, but there were two others who came into place as well. They were taller humanlike figures. Their faces looked more like skulls with a thin layer of skin. They had razor sharp teeth and claws and red eyes.

Stephen grudgingly got back into bed, but he was too excited to sleep. He stared at the key. It was one of those old-fashioned skeleton keys with ornate swirls on one end. He tried to remember everything he'd seen and heard - the creatures, the colors, Elyon. And when he got back, there were the words floating in mid-air from the page and something about battles? As he was thinking about everything he'd experienced, he drifted off to sleep.

Stephen had forgotten about Belshazzon who quietly stood in the corner. Belshazzon wasn't alone; he was able to summon more beings from Elyon's realm with just a whisper. He knew what was ahead of Stephen. The other beings Belshazzon had called had human forms. They were all dressed in battle gear. This was just the beginning.

Lemachor sensed something. To him, it was an unwelcome presence. He had been barking out orders to his soldiers so much that he wasn't paying attention. When he looked up, he saw his arch nemesis, Belshazzon.

"Marchon!" Lemachor yelled, and one of the creatures appeared instantly by his side. "You must go to Gravinder at once."

3

Gravinder was the lord of the dark kingdom who named his race of slaves, the Gravine, after himself. He'd once been a trusted adviser in Elyon's kingdom, serving as the highest ranking Enkeli, the race of human-like creatures who lived in Elyon's land, but that wasn't enough for him. Gravinder despised Elyon for his compassion on this group of humans that he'd rescued and called his own. Elyon cared for them and would come to their aid, in spite of the fact that many would then forget his kindness only to make some of the same mistakes again. Gravinder couldn't understand why Elyon would desire their company when Elyon had the Enkeli with him all the time. In that race were skilled musicians and artisans. The Enkeli were beautiful, and they weren't weak-minded like the humans as Gravinder saw them. He saw Elyon as weak as well and inferior to Gravinder because Elyon cared for them so deeply. Gravinder wanted to destroy all the humans. So Gravinder plotted to oust Elyon from the place he thought he should inhabit. When Elyon heard of Gravinder's plot, he banished him to the outermost parts of Elyon's realm. In its caverns of the icy blackness, there was no sun to shine to bring light or warmth. It was always cold, always dark. The move into the frigid realm had changed the appearance of Gravinder. While he was still in Elyon's kingdom, he looked like Elyon and Belshazzon. He was tall and muscular. But once banished, his beauty and eternal youth disappeared. He and the Gravine began to look like the centuries-old creatures they really were. Gravinder's real appearance was laughable and pathetic. He was only about two feet tall and weighed about 40 pounds. His skin was shriveled and a sickly yellow; he had no teeth or hair. When he was first banished, he hid himself from those who plotted with him so they couldn't see what the banishment cost him. He knew he couldn't command his armies if they saw him as he really looked. Although most of his special abilities had been stripped away, he retained his intellect and his ability to manipulate others. He learned he could create an illusion so his armies never saw what Elyon had reduced him to. He used this to his advantage, creating any appearance he wanted. This also worked when he wanted to torment the humans, who were now his primary enemy. He couldn't defeat Elyon so he focused on bringing pain and destruction to Elyon's people.

To his armies and enemies, he projected a fierce image. He stood over nine-feet tall, and his skin was a vivid burnt orange. His arms and chest had bulky, rippling muscles. His legs were thick like tree trunks. At the ends of his fingers were sharp claws. His head was shaped like a ram with horns. He had no eyes to speak of just shafts of yellow light piercing through eye sockets. He had sharp fangs. His voice was deep and guttural. The soldiers in his army trembled at the sight of him. Fear was one of the greatest weapons he had.

The Gravine also changed in appearance after their banishment. Over time, Gravinder got bored with them and experimented on their appearance. He learned how to manipulate matter when he entered Earth, and he practiced these techniques on his own subjects. He enjoyed the pain it brought them. He also hated his own subjects; they had failed him in overthrowing Elyon.

Marchon crawled into Gravinder's presence and waited before Gravinder's throne. He was sure he would receive some punishment for the news he was about to bring, but like all of the Gravine, he was unable to die.

Gravinder closed his eyelids to a tiny slit as he gazed upon Marchon. He knew his coming meant bad news. None of the Gravine were to leave their station unless it meant Elyon was on the move.

"You know what your presence here means, Marchon?" growled Gravinder.

"Yes, my lord," Marchon said without looking up.

"How have you failed me?" Gravinder asked as his voice got louder.

"The boy," Marchon started and trembled. "He traveled through the book to meet with Elyon."

"No," Gravinder screamed.

Gravinder motioned to two guards standing in his frozen chambers.

One of them ran his sword through Marchon as they carried him out of the room toward his place of eternal torture. Marchon's screams could be heard for the next few moments as Gravinder realized it was time to put a plan into motion. He'd been ready for this for many years. He knew the ancient prophecies. He would have to destroy the family to keep the prophecies from coming to pass.

"Belek and Bestian," Gravinder roared.

Instantly, the two Gravine appeared and groveled before their evil king.

"Yes sir," they replied in unison, their eyes fixed on the floor beneath his feet.

"The family of this man named John has been a thorn in my side for centuries. Lemachor had the problem contained for a short time, but now, you know what must be done," he said. "You finish what he started, and don't let me see you again."

As quickly as they appeared, they vanished from Gravinder's presence.

"Leave me alone," he yelled to the other guards standing in the room.

Gravinder walked over to a curtain and angrily tore it back. Behind it was a six foot tall hourglass. Although there was no sand visible in the top portion of the hourglass, there was still a steady stream pouring through the narrow opening into the bottom portion, and the sand level below never changed. Gravinder stared at it. And then in a rage, Gravinder grabbed the curtain and flung it back into place.

Yes, time was short, and only Elyon knew how exactly how much time was left.

Belek and Bestian sped from Gravinder's frozen kingdom into Stephen and John's home, in order to assist Lemachor and the others. Obviously, this was a serious situation. Lemachor had been on this assignment for several generations of Stephen's family and neutralized them. Their ancestors had been highly effective in defeating Gravinder's plans and paving the way for Elyon to establish his kingdom on Earth until Lemachor arrived. They had been a force to be reckoned with, but the past few generations had weakened. Now all that stood between Gravinder's efforts to destroy the human race and thwart Elyon's plans was one 12 year-old boy and possibly, his 55 year-old grandfather.

Belek and Bestian arrived in the house to find Lemachor standing in the hallway blocking a doorway. He seemed frozen in place, and they quickly realized why. Lemachor's gaze was fixed ahead of him. They stood fixed in place and in silence with swords drawn against their longtime enemies with Belshazzon at the lead.

It had been many years since Lemachor had seen Belshazzon. Even though, he dressed in all black in a fashion that Stephen was drawn to, there was no mistaking Belshazzon. While he was one of Elyon's finest warriors, he rarely left Elyon's kingdom. There were numerous other Enkeli soldiers who fought on the side of the humans.

Lemachor laughed to try and mask his fear.

"Belshazzon. Babysitting duty, I see," Lemachor taunted. "Why has such a high-ranking Enkeli as you been kicked out of Elyon's courts and into this earthly realm to babysit this child – not even a man – not even a man of importance?"

He cackled.

"What did you do wrong?" Lemachor continued. "Elyon have a

bad day?"

Lemachor hated Belshazzon because it was on the end of Belshazzon's blade that Lemachor was forced out of Elyon's kingdom. This was a particularly unpleasant memory for Lemachor. He really didn't want to be part of the rebellion. He felt he had been tricked by another Gravine named Bandion.

"So you have to get your hands dirty now, don't you? Wiping the nose of a baby," Lemachor continued to mock Belshazzon. "

Belshazzon didn't show any emotion. He simply stared at Lemachor and waited for him to finish his ranting.

"Is that the best you can do? After thousands of earth years, and that's all you can say?" Belshazzon replied. "You and I both had a choice to make. We both know who made the right choice, now don't we?"

The remark sliced through Lemachor, who hated Gravinder for all his false promises. Lemachor would have rather been in Elyon's courts instead of this earthly realm in Gravinder's grip. In the realm of the Enkeli and Gravine, there was no time as human beings understand it. For them to stand there was like the blink of an eye.

While Lemachor taunted, Stephen slept a few more hours. It wasn't long before the sun spilled across Stephen's face nudging him from his sleep. He felt groggy from the previous night's adventure. Even as he slept, he felt the adventure continue. In his dreams, he saw Elyon and all of the wonderful creatures in his kingdom. He vaguely remembered talking with Elyon in his dream and wondered if Elyon gave him more instructions. He couldn't remember, but he did know he needed to get to that book.

Surely, in all those pages, there were answers to his questions? He quickly put on a pair of blue jeans and a sweatshirt and headed out his bedroom door. As he walked down the hall, he didn't notice all of the Enkeli battle ready and standing in formation at first. He walked through their neat lines until he got to where Belshazzon stood. When he reached Belshazzon, Stephen turned and saw the Enkeli. He slowly did a 360 degree turn. His eyes grew wide, and his mouth dropped.

"Where did they all come from?" he thought.

His first instinct was to run. As he finished his rotation, Lemachor and the Gravine ahead of him came into full view.

"Don't be afraid," Belshazzon said. "They're here to help you."

Stephen saw the Gravine blocking the door of the room that he wanted to enter. He remembered the words that floated out of the pages that he wasn't going to be fighting against other people, but his enemies would be from different realms. How was he supposed to fight them? He didn't even have a weapon.

All of a sudden, Stephen heard his own voice.

"In the name of Elyon, move out of my way!" he ordered.

At once, the Enkeli and the Gravine moved into action. Swords drawn, they charged at one another. The Enkeli's swords weren't like the Gravine's. More light. It seemed to be a theme of Elyon's kingdom. Their swords had jeweled handles and blades of light. They flew above Stephen's head, fiercely engaged. In an odd way, it was like a slow-motion dance as the pairs of very different swordsmen flung their weapons at each other. They instinctively moved, blocking blows. Sometimes, they locked together, but neither side seemed to be gaining any ground.

Stephen stood and stared. He felt paralyzed as he watched them fighting. He began to remember parts of his dream. Elyon was speaking to him. He told Stephen that the Enkeli received power when they heard the words of Elyon even if they weren't coming directly from Elyon. The book contained the answers. The words in the book contained the life force. Stephen really had to get to that book.

Again, he spoke the name of Elyon, and the Enkeli surged against the Gravine taking the upper hand. The light pierced through the Gravine's flesh, burning it. Many of the Gravine retreated. While they could be injured, they could not be killed. Their wounds would quickly heal, but they had to retreat in order to mend.

Stephen realized this was his chance as the Enkeli were making the distraction he needed to move the Gravine out of the doorway. He burst down the hall. He was almost in the room when he fell to the ground. He looked down at his ankles, but he didn't see anything at first. He closed his eyes and opened them again and saw Bestian's claws digging into them. Stephen screamed in pain as the grasp tightened, and his heart began beating wildly. In his head, he kept hearing Belshazzon say to not be afraid. He closed his eyes, concentrated on getting in the room and struggled to crawl. He could hear the noise of the swords above him. He looked up and saw Belshazzon's light blade engaged with Lemachor's sword. He paused for a moment wondering how light could make a sound. As he did, Bestian's claws further penetrated into Stephen's ankle, causing him to cry out in more pain.

"In the name of Elyon, let me go," Stephen screamed.

Immediately, one of the other Enkeli grabbed Bestian and threw him against the wall. Stephen crawled into the room and closed the door behind him. He looked down at his ankles. They were both bleeding and throbbing with pain. He didn't know what to do, but he didn't want to risk going back into the fray outside the door. As he sat by the door for a moment, he tried to catch his breath and wait for his heart rate to return to normal.

Outside the door, Lemachor and the other Gravine retreated, granting the Enkeli a minor victory. They vanished, but it was only temporary. They would bide their time until there was a better time for an attack. If anything, they were persistent, never seeing any type of defeat or victory as final.

Meanwhile, Stephen remembered the words floating from the pages of the book. "I guess I know what you were trying to tell me this morning," he whispered as he tried to ignore the pain in his ankles from Bestian's claws.

He got up to read the book, but it wasn't there. He limped over to the table. There was a book on the table, but this one was smaller than the one he saw the night before. He could pick this one up and move it.

What happened?

"The book has amazing abilities," said a voice behind him.

Stephen turned around. John had come into the room and had made his way to the table.

"But it was huge last night. How did you get past all those things in the hallway?" Stephen asked and pointed to his bleeding ankles. "They attacked me, and they were flying through the air and fighting with this really big dude named Belshazzon. He is my protector, according to Elyon. The ones with Belshazzon are ripped and strong. The others are like ugly monsters. I've never seen anything so ugly, and they smell awful - like rotten eggs."

Stephen sat back on the floor for a minute. He felt overwhelmed.

"The book opened for you to go through a portal from this realm to the realm where Elyon lives. It made a way for you to get to him. I've never seen it do that before, but my grandfather told me about the book. I wanted to go with you, but I was afraid," John said.

"And for those creatures in the hallways - those are part of a group of creatures called the Gravine," he continued. "I saw you get away from them. They weren't really concerned with me. Once you made it into the room, they left. Not forever, though, they'll be back. That's just the way they are."

"They looked like something out of a horror movie," Stephen said.

"Those are the enemy of Elyon, and now that you've taken your place, they hate you too."

"Great. Just great. Kids at school already don't like me, and now, I've got these gargoyle-looking things with claws after me. I thought it was going to tear my ankles off."

"That's only half of what they'd like to do. They'd love to kill you, Stephen."

Stephen felt a chill when his grandfather said that. John pulled a chair in front of the book and motioned for Stephen to do the same.

"The Gravine were once Enkeli – those are the ones who were fighting for you, but they wanted power. An Enkeli named Gravinder who was close to Elyon, decided just being an Enkeli wasn't enough. He felt he was better than Elyon, and he wanted to take Elyon's place," John explained. "That got him kicked out of the Jeweled City where Elyon lives. "

As he was talking, John reached down to Stephen's bleeding ankles. He took a handkerchief out of his pocket and wrapped it around Stephen's left ankle. He placed both hands around the ankle. Stephen felt an electric current go through his ankle and jumped. Then, his grandfather's hands began to heat up. Stephen stared at John as he wiped the blood away, and when he removed the handkerchief, the bleeding had stopped. He did the same thing for Stephen's right ankle.

"Whoa," Stephen shook his head and glanced at his grandfather. "How did you do that?"

Stephen bent over to take a closer look at his ankles. There wasn't even the slightest scratch even though Bestian's claws had dug deep into Stephen's flesh.

John didn't answer the question.

"It's time for this book to become what it was intended to be, a doorway into another realm and a portal to knowledge and understanding, not a trophy to be stared at," John said.

"I had gashes in my ankles, and they were bleeding. Now they aren't, and they don't hurt any more. And they look normal." Stephen wasn't paying any attention to John. He couldn't figure out what had happened. "What did you do?"

John smiled and shook his head.

"There's no time for explanations. We have to get busy."

Stephen stopped looking at his ankles and looked up at his grandfather. Stephen hadn't noticed it until then, but his grandfather looked different this morning. Stephen had always thought of him as a really old man, but today, his hair seemed darker not that he had a lot of gray to begin with.

Did he dye his hair last night? What was different about him?

He didn't look so old today. The wrinkles around his eyes

didn't seem so deep, and he wasn't as sad today. He looked taller or something. Stephen wasn't sure what it was. And he was sure there was a glow to his skin. This was weird because Stephen was not into noticing whether someone's skin had a glow to it. He wasn't good at guessing people's ages either because everyone seemed old to him, but his grandfather looked less ancient.

So much had transpired over the night that Stephen realized his grandfather had no clue what he'd been through; there hadn't been any time to tell him.

"You said you were afraid to go into the book? Why? It's the most wonderful place ever," Stephen said. The excitement of his adventure showed in his voice. It began to spill out of it. He couldn't sit. He started pacing the floor as he described what he'd seen.

"Papa, it was awesome. I've never seen anything like it. I walked up to the book, and I couldn't keep my balance. I felt like I was falling. I couldn't stop myself. It was almost like the book was a giant hole, and I fell in. But I didn't fall in. I fell up. It was flying," he said, gesturing wildly.

He clamped his hands on top of his head for a moment and sat on a chair. He paused. He couldn't believe the words coming out of his mouth. It all seemed too incredible.

"Then, I ended up in the most beautiful place in the world. Well, I guess it wasn't in the world because it was nothing like I'd seen here. It was crazy – wow," he said.

John fixed his gaze on Stephen as he told his story. John smiled because he remembered his grandfather telling him similar stories of generations past. Neither John nor John's father had been through the portal. It had been many generations since something like this had happened even though they knew it was possible and hoped it would come. Stephen told him about the creatures in Elyon's world, and he spoke of Elyon himself.

"He's a king. He's powerful. I should've been afraid to be running in like that and volunteering to help him. And his guards – whoa. They were huge. They were scary looking, but they weren't scary. I know that doesn't make any sense. I think they could've killed me just by looking at me, but they didn't. And then there were these fiery creatures. I don't know how to describe those. They were flames, but they didn't burn anything. I felt like I belonged there. I felt like I'd known Elyon all my life even though I'd never met him," Stephen said.

Stephen paused. He had to catch his breath because he talked so fast from the excitement.

"The place you are speaking about is called the Jeweled City, and it's Elyon's home. You know you might want to write this down because you could forget it."

"I could never forget this."

"Small details are easily forgotten," said John as he moved toward a desk in the library. He pulled a leather bound book out of one of the drawers and handed it to Stephen. "Put as much as you can remember down on paper. When you read it later, it will stay fresh and real to you. Trust me, in a lifetime, there are so many things that happen - so many things it's easy to forget."

Stephen looked at the book. He guessed it made sense, but he knew he would never forget.

"So you believe me then?" asked Stephen, who was still pinching himself to see if he might have been making some of it up. "You don't think I'm crazy or lying?"

"I have no doubt that you experienced what you said you did. Stephen, I realize that I haven't been the best grandfather I could be. You have a destiny, and I need to help you fulfill it. Until now, I have ignored it, but I've been wrong to do that."

Stephen was quiet.

"I believe you because I've heard the same stories you just told," he said. He stood up and walked over to the bookshelf. There were volumes of leather bound books on it. "Do you see these books? Many of your ancestors wrote in journals about their experiences as keeper of the book."

Stephen looked at the many books in the room.

"These will give you some insight too, but they can never replace that book. They will help you though because there will be a lot of times you'll think you are going crazy. You will see things others can't. You will do things others can't do," John continued. "For too long, I've been quiet. I realized yesterday that I've been blind. No, I think it's more like I've been dead, walking around in a body but having no purpose or direction. I don't know how I walked away from the path my parents and grandparents cut for me. They taught me so many things. I experienced so much, but nothing like what you've already experienced. It's almost like a dream to me, the years before…"

His voice choked and trailed off for a minute.

"I forgot them for many years. Last night, everything came back to me. While I may have failed to do everything I was supposed to do up until now, it's not too late. I know it's not too late because some of the gifts Elyon gave are still there. When I touched you and your ankle was healed. I haven't seen that happen in so long. I'll be here to help you."

"You look different today, Papa," said Stephen. "I don't know what it is about you."

Stephen saw his grandfather's eyes. He'd never noticed them before, but they flashed like the stars twinkling in the night sky.

John smiled.

"Elyon's people are scattered all over the earth. You are one of those who will gather them together. Elyon plans to set up a new kingdom for them, and he will be doing it soon. You will know Elyon's followers because of what you see in me. Elyon is the king of the light, and there is light in his people. It won't be like people have a tattoo or wear a sign. You just know it when you are around it. It's like you will be able to sense it," he said. "You should be able to see his light in them."

Just then, Stephen remembered the key Elyon had given to him. He had stuffed it in his jeans' pocket.

"Elyon gave this to me. Do you know what this is for?" asked Stephen as he removed it.

John took the golden key from Stephen and stared at it for a moment. The top portion was a series or intertwined circles and swirls, and it appeared to be made of pure gold. There was a ruby in its center. It was inscribed in cursive script with the words "Nothing is impossible." Like everything Elyon touched, the key seemed to be illuminated. There was not light shining directly on it, but the key acted as a reflector. John wracked his brain to think of any time his parents or grandparents had told him about a key. Nothing came to mind right away.

"I'm not sure," he said. "We'll find out."

John handed the key back to Stephen.

"We should find a safe place for that. I know it's important."

Stephen took it back, and the pair turned their attention to the book.

4

After spending the day with Stephen, John couldn't sleep. Like Stephen, he was overwhelmed. He went to his retreat – his workshop, where he turned on the radio. His workshop was always a place he could relax and focus. Over the years, its contents had evolved. Many of his early inventions were mechanical, but as technology increased, he found himself developing computer programs and technology. He took college courses mainly online because he didn't like to leave the house, but he loved learning. As he sat at his desk, he realized all he'd been doing was running away, filling his life with things that really meant nothing to him. All of it was so empty.

He stared at his hands. Despite not having used the healing gift at all in recent years, he had instinctively put them on Stephen's ankles and expected them to be instantly healed. He wondered how it was possible that the gift forgotten and unused still worked? He hadn't even thought about the things he'd seen in the past.

His journal was not in the library with the journals of his ancestors. He felt it didn't belong there. They wrote of the many incredible things they'd seen during their lives. A healing such as Stephen's was small in comparison with some of the other stories he'd read and heard his father tell. His journal was in a desk drawer inside his shop. He pulled it out and thumbed through the pages. It had been many years since he'd written anything in it. He didn't have anything to write.

How could I have forgotten? he thought.

Over the past several hours, John had started to see things in a different light. He felt like a pair of dark glasses had been removed from his eyes. There were so many things in his life he blamed on others; he blamed on Elyon when John himself could have made things turn out differently.

He remembered the night Aaron left. Things had been building for a while. Aaron wanted to go to school far away, but John wanted him to stay closer for a year or two. Then there was a motorcycle Aaron wanted, but John felt a motorcycle was too dangerous for a teen who had just learned to drive. It was all such a stupid argument. Underneath it all, John was afraid. He'd lost all the people he'd loved in his life. Aaron was all he had left. Aaron earned his own money, and he bought a motorcycle against his father's wishes. That night, on his way home, Aaron had an accident. He was fine just a few bumps and bruises. The motorcycle was fine, but John was afraid of something worse happening to Aaron. When Aaron came inside that night, they argued again.

"Why can't you let me make my own decisions?" Aaron asked.

"I only want what's best for you," John replied.

"No, you just want to control me and my life. I can't be what you think I should. I don't know what I want to do with my life, but I'm not staying here. I want to see the world. I want to do great things. I was made for more than this," Aaron said and headed for this room.

Looking back, it really didn't seem as fierce as it did that night. The next morning, John got up, and Aaron was gone with a note that simply said, *"I want to live my life my way."*

As tears streamed down his face, John pulled the note out of his journal where it had been folded and tucked away for all those years. So many times, he had thought about trying to find Aaron, but instead of searching for his son, he waited for Aaron to return, just as he'd waited for Meredith to return. He'd allowed his own pride to come in the way of his relationship with his son.

"I've been so wrong," he whispered. "I'm so sorry."

At that moment, he heard the words of a song being played on the radio. They were singing about second chances.

"This is such a great responsibility," John said out loud. "I failed Aaron, but I'm not going to fail Stephen. I'm going to fulfill it this time, but I need help. I can't do this alone."

As he sat in his workshop, John was oblivious to what was taking place through the veil into the other realm. For decades, the Gravine forces surrounding John's house were relatively dormant, but as John spoke, several Enkeli, in full battle gear entered the room. The Gravine, who had mainly been watchers, now found themselves under the swords of Enkeli. They had come to assist John as he accepted the call to teach Stephen. The Gravine had a stronghold for too long. Many battles would lie ahead.

Part of the terms of Gravinder's exile was for him never to return to the Jeweled City and to never interfere in Elyon's affairs; however, Gravinder had repeatedly violated these terms when it came to the human beings. Elyon considered them a top priority under "his affairs."

Gravinder had many schemes when it came to the humans. He felt they were weak and inferior to him. His best secret was to remain undetected in the lives of the humans. He thought they had weak brains; they thought they were so smart, but they couldn't figure out it was his minions who planted thoughts into their minds – thoughts of hopelessness and despair. Through Gravinder's tactics, many lives were destroyed. The Gravine had brought down governments because of misconceptions and distrust. They'd ruined marriages and relationships between parents and children. They plotted violence against the human race, and it was often easy to pit people against each other letting them kill one another. They could prey on human minds easily unless a keeper of the book shared the secrets contained within it. It gave detailed plans and strategies on how to keep Gravinder at bay. But it sounded far-fetched to many who heard about it. After all, it was written about something they couldn't see.

Gravinder considered himself a genius. He even felt his intellect was superior to Elyon; after all, Elyon had pity and compassion on these weak humans so Elyon must be inferior. In reality, the fact that Elyon had defeated Gravinder and continued to thwart his plans was proof of Elyon's superior power. Since Gravinder had broken the terms of the agreement, there was a permanent punishment on the horizon for his high treason and the Gravine who joined him. They would be forever locked and bound in chains they could not break, and they would then be tormented with the same types of pain Gravinder had afflicted on Elyon's people.

Gravinder had also spent centuries of his exile creating physical weapons against the human beings. He could manipulate matter and learned how to mutate bacteria and viruses. He'd introduced many unexplained and incurable diseases into human beings over time and took great pleasure in seeing them die slow, painful deaths.

Gravinder wanted to keep those ancient prophecies from being fulfilled, and he'd almost convinced himself he could win against Elyon because he'd tasted so many victories over them. Only Elyon knew when this appointed time was, and human beings would have a part in the plan to end Gravinder's kingdom. He gave Gravinder the hourglass as a constant reminder his time would come to an end. On one hand, it was unsettling to Gravinder to find that Stephen was beginning to fulfill some of those ancient texts, and that he could be one of those humans used to bring about his eternal downfall. But they'd won so many victories; Gravinder's pride only swelled more. As he sat in his frozen lair, he laughed at the thought of a 12 year-old boy having the ability to defeat him; however, he knew he couldn't be too careful. If Elyon saw something in this child, he needed to investigate. He summoned Lemachor from the home.

Lemachor bowed and trembled in his presence.

"What is the report on this boy?" Gravinder asked.

"Since going into the portal, he has returned to study the book along with his grandfather, sir," Lemachor said, omitting the fact that Stephen had had a minor victory when he used Elyon's name to give the Enkeli power so Stephen could get back into the room.

"And what are you doing to stop him?" Gravinder growled.

"Well, we have a plan to use the same things that have always worked down through the ages. It's only been a few hours. We are certain this excitement will be short-lived, and like most boys, he will lose interest. We are working on distractions for him to help the excitement fade away. We also plan to bring back all those painful memories for the grandfather."

"I'm also hearing other rumors I don't like."

Lemachor didn't want to know what was coming next.

"Who from the Enkeli is protecting the boy?" asked Gravinder as he narrowed the eye slits.

"Belshazzon, my lord."

Lemachor turned his gaze down as he whispered the name, bracing for Gravinder's wrath. Belshazzon was second on the list when it came to those Gravinder hated. Before Gravinder's exile, he and Belshazzon were like brothers and highly trusted by the king. At one time, here was no need for warriors or fighting in the Jeweled City, but that soon changed. Gravinder tried to turn Belshazzon's allegiance to him instead of Elyon, promising him power and position. Belshazzon would have been Gravinder's right-hand. Belshazzon was loyal to Elyon. He exposed Gravinder's plan to Elyon and led the effort to banish him. Gravinder soon found Belshazzon to be a worthy adversary when it came to the sword, and the weapons Elyon had given the Enkeli could cause a lot of damage. Although the Gravine couldn't die, they could experience intense pain.

Gravinder's last images of the Jeweled City were of Belshazzon's blade of light and Elyon's face. Gravinder couldn't erase Elyon's expression from his memory. It wasn't rage, but the sadness from the betrayal of a close and trusted friend. Gravinder tried to dismiss it as weakness, but the vision tormented him. "Belshazzon," repeated Gravinder as he walked over to the hourglass. Over the past few hours, there seemed to be less sand running through the opening. Borrowed time, even it would end at some point. With less and less sand dripping through, could this be a sign?

"Don't wait, and turn up your efforts. Time is short. We have to keep Elyon's plan from coming into effect. He can't defeat me again – surely not at the hands of a little boy," he said.

An eternity of payback was not something Gravinder was looking forward to. "Yes, my lord," said Lemachor as he bowed and left.

5

The next morning Stephen sighed as he got ready for school. He was sad the amazing weekend had ended. Now it was back to reality - whatever that meant. Stephen wasn't looking forward to it. When he walked downstairs, he found his grandfather still wearing his bathrobe and drinking a cup of coffee at the kitchen table.

"Why aren't you dressed yet? Aren't you driving me to school today?" Stephen asked.

"There's been a change in plans," said John. "I will be going to the school district office today. From now on, you will be taking classes over the computer at home. You will be able to go at a faster pace academically, and this will free up your time."

"Cool."

That didn't bother him at all. Stephen did well academically, but he wasn't interested in playing sports and didn't know anything about football or baseball. Sports were the most important thing among the other students where Stephen went to school. Stephen was not athletically inclined. He tried to ignore it, but he didn't like being the outcast. Kids called him names.

Stephen enjoyed reading, and he loved to spend time in his grandfather's workshop. He could spend hours taking something apart just to see how it worked and to see if he could put it back together. He especially loved his grandfather's old cars. The two of them often worked on the cars together. But Stephen had an artistic side as well and loved to sketch. In a way his artwork and his love of machines were related. He paid a lot of attention to small details and made sure every line and curve was perfectly placed.

When they weren't working on machines together, Stephen and John spent a lot of time fishing on a nearby pond. Fishing was another hobby the two enjoyed together. Stephen thought those were the times when his grandfather seemed the happiest.

As he thought about his grandfather's comment, Stephen was happy to be homeschooled. There would be more adventures in the book, and he didn't want to miss out on any of that by having to be in a classroom all the time.

Stephen headed down the hall. No unexplained chills, no visions of monster-like creatures and no fighting to get down the hallway. No claws in his ankles either. This was a good sign.

"Well, I guess I don't have to worry about them anymore," Stephen thought as he passed a faint shadow at his grandfather's bedroom door.

Stephen wasn't paying attention. If he had, he would have seen multiple pairs of eyes on him as he walked down the hall. Lemachor didn't move until he was sure the boy had passed him completely. His warriors waited at the other end of the hallway. Belshazzon also watched, and Stephen seemed oblivious to his presence as well. He was focused on getting to the book. Once inside the room, he thumbed through the pages. Despite the fact that it was written in a language he didn't understand, Stephen could read it with ease. With each word, he remembered the taste of the scroll in his mouth.

Through the book, he learned about Gravinder's expulsion out of the Jeweled City and his ultimate punishment. He also learned that no matter what Gravinder or the Gravine did to him, Stephen had the ultimate victory. Circumstances might say differently, but Elyon would always prevail if Stephen allowed it and followed the principles. As a follower of Elyon, Stephen had a legal right to Elyon's power and authority. Elyon had defeated Gravinder centuries before, and he plainly gave this power of attorney to his followers. Where

Stephen had seen this twinkle in his grandfather's eyes and radiance in his face, the Gravine saw as a red light around the individual. There was also something else the Gravine saw, it was like a brand upon their skin that identified them as one of Elyon's own.

Unfortunately, not many knew of this power they had received. They allowed themselves to be tormented by Gravinder's plans, and many times, they suffered and died without ever knowing the benefits of being part of Elyon's family. Stephen saw his task as daunting. He knew that part of what Elyon brought him to the Jeweled City to tell him was he needed to help bring his people together. He had to find them and anyone else who wanted to join.

Stephen still found it hard to believe that he had something big to do with his life. It was scary for him to think that this king was entrusting him with a task. Stephen found himself getting sleepy. There was a window seat in the library, and Stephen took one of the journals off the shelf. He tried to continue reading there, but soon, he was fast asleep.

When Stephen opened his eyes, he was far from the window seat in the library.

He looked around. He'd seen pictures of Africa in books. Where he was looked like those pictures. There were some trees in the distance, but Stephen was walking on dirt. He saw huts with thatched roofs, but where were the people?

Soon he realized where they were. He could hear people crying, and there was muffled talking. He headed toward the sounds. They were coming from inside one of the huts. As he approached the hut, he saw some people standing near the door. They were crying too. He looked around. There were women holding babies, and men standing outside huts. They stared at Stephen.

He didn't stop to try to communicate with them. He didn't have to speak to know what was going on. He just knew. He could feel their pain. Their grief was overwhelming. He opened the door to the hut, and he walked in. No one stopped him. There, ahead of him on a cot was a boy about the same age as Stephen, but his body was thin, wracked with disease and the effects of hunger. There were flies around his lips. There was little muscle tone in his slender arms and legs. People were crying loudly. They looked up at Stephen, and Stephen could see into their eyes. He knew just as his grandfather said he would know. These were some of Elyon's people.

Stephen wanted to do something to help these people, but what could he possibly do to save a dead child? And he knew that this child's family was looking to him to help them. He remembered what John had done to his ankles a few days before, and he knew what to do. He walked over to the bed where the child was lying and grabbed his lifeless hand. The boy's eyes were closed, and his lips were slightly opened. Stephen leaned over the boy's face.

"In the name of Elyon, live," he said.

Immediately, the boy gasped for breath and coughed, and his eyes flew open. More than that, his frail body began to fill out. He was no longer emaciated. He looked well-nourished. He didn't resemble the boy Stephen had seen lying on the mat. Stephen turned to the boy's mother and father. He knew that the father was the leader of the people, and he said "Elyon is returning for you soon. He has heard you."

Even though, he spoke in English, the father nodded as though he understood. The boy's mother grabbed the boy and hugged him, crying louder than she had before. Stephen walked outside and noticed it was raining. The parched land drank the water as soon as it hit. The people outside were still crying, but their faces reflected a joy because of the rain.

Stephen opened his eyes. He was back in his house and lying on the window seat. He sat up and looked around the room.

"That was some dream I just had, Papa," he said as he arose from the window seat and walked over to his grandfather who was seated at his desk. "I was in a village in Africa, and there was a dead child there. His family was part of Elyon's people. I could tell just like you said I would. There was something about their eyes. I told the boy to live, and he got up."

Stephen shook his head.

"I guess I've been reading too many of these old books. I'm starting to dream about the stuff they wrote about doing," he said.

He looked at his grandfather who had not spoken a word.

"What?" Stephen asked.

He saw his grandfather looking at Stephen's feet.

"What is on your socks and pants?"

They looked down. His blue jean cuff and his white socks were covered with mud.

"It wasn't a dream, was it?" Stephen asked as he touched his wet pants' leg.

"No, Stephen, it wasn't. It was as real as your trip into the Jeweled City," John said. "This is going to be normal for you. Uniting people from around the world isn't going to be an easy task, and it would require enormous amounts of time and money. Elyon works on another dimension. Time and distance mean nothing to him, and at times, they will mean nothing to you."

Lemachor paced outside the library. They'd spent too much time locked away with the book. He had to come up with a way to keep them out of that room. Knowledge was indeed power, and the more the two of them knew about Gravinder and his plans, the worse it was for Lemachor and the Gravine. Unlike Gravinder, the Gravine had no idea of the hourglass Elyon had given. They didn't know how short time was. They knew of their eternal punishment, but it had been so many centuries since Elyon had imposed the sentence, they'd almost forgotten. They believed Elyon had grown soft, and maybe, he'd forgotten what he said as well.

"The boy isn't in school so there are no distractions there we can use against him," Lemachor said to Bestian. "He has always enjoyed reading so getting him away from the book is difficult."

"What about pitting the boy against his grandfather?" suggested Bestian. "It worked with the man and his son. It could work again. And there's always pride or discouragement. I particularly like the last two. I've seen more defeat in the lives of these humans using those two."

"Yes, those are ones that always work," Lemachor said. "The problem lies with Belshazzon. He's there watching over this one. Now that he's there, he won't leave. He's stronger than we are. We need to be able to get close to the boy, but the boy has seen us. He can't know that it's us making suggestions; he has to think it is him thinking these things. Of course, you know all this. It's worked time and time again. But it's getting rather boring. We need some new plots, but until then, we have to call in some reinforcements. There aren't enough of us here to win especially if the boy gets stronger and learns he can fuel Belshazzon's strength with the life force in the book."

"I will get your reinforcements," said Bestian.

Lemachor nodded at him and then whispered, "Be quiet about all of this. A sneak attack is called for, and Belshazzon can't be the wiser."

Bestian vanished as Lemachor made his plan. Fear tactics were always good for a laugh for the Gravine, but they also provided a valuable service. Lemachor left the door of the library and reappeared in his attic lair, where the plotting began. Belshazzon quietly watched. He knew the Gravine's lack of activity could only mean they were in preparation mode.

Fear was a major weapon in the Gravine's arsenal, and they'd studied Stephen enough to know snakes were the only thing Stephen was really afraid of. His family's home was on several acres of land in eastern Georgia with towering pine trees and several ponds. He and his grandfather would spend spring and summer days hiking through the woods and fishing. They often saw wildlife on their outings. There were white tail deer, beavers, various birds and snakes. Most of the time they were hidden from view, but a sunny day would bring them out to bask in the rays. Snakes were fine until the day when one got caught on Stephen's fishing line when he was reeling it in. Stephen was about 5 at the time, and the snake seemed enormous to him. John told him it was a cottonmouth, and those were dangerous. When John saw the snake on the end of the line, he took his pocketknife and cut the line. Stephen thought he'd almost touched it, and from then on, Stephen was afraid of snakes.

It didn't keep them from going out into the woods, but Stephen was cautious of where he stepped. He kept his eyes focused on the path so as not to encounter one. If he saw one sunning itself on a rock, he stayed as far away from it as possible.

Stephen wasn't outside on this occasion. He was walking through a dimly lit corridor. He called to his grandfather, but there was no answer. As he walked through the corridor, he looked down. At his feet, there were hundreds of slithering snakes. He tried to scream, but nothing came out. They wrapped their bodies around his leg, and he saw their mouths open. They were just like he remembered with only white showing from inside their mouths. They began to suffocate him. No, these weren't pythons. How could they do this?

Stephen woke up gasping for breath. The nightmare was all too real especially when he awoke to find Lemachor's hands around his throat, and two other Gravine holding his body in place. One had his hand over Stephen's mouth. Stephen couldn't scream, and he was having problems breathing.

At the same time, Belshazzon was fighting off three other Gravine who had jumped into the room all at once. Belshazzon had two glimmering swords of light, one in each hand. He ferociously wielded each blade and performed a series of jumps and kicks as he fought the Gravine trio.

One of the blades cut through the Gravine; he screamed, but there was no blood, only a wretched, putrid smell that permeated the room. He vanished, returning to the ice caves to heal.

"Don't be afraid of them," Belshazzon called out to Stephen as he concentrated on the last two Gravine. "One of their greatest weapons is fear."

The Gravine were no match for Belshazzon's blade of light as it tore through their flesh. They retreated once they saw Belshazzon had gained the upper hand. Now Belshazzon needed to get them off of Stephen who was thrashing in his bed trying to gasp for air and scream all at the same time. Stephen was finally able to yell, and John heard him from across the hall. He sprung out of bed to find out what was happening. As he opened the door, John could see Belshazzon fighting Lemachor. They had risen above the bed and walked on air as they threw their swords at each other.

"In the name of Elyon, you must leave," John shouted.

Lemachor's sword fell from his hands at those words. The grip the two other Gravine had on Stephen lessened, but they didn't want to give up quite yet.

"At the name of Elyon, you must go," John said again in a lower and more authoritative tone this time.

Shafts of light ripped through the three Gravine in unison. Their tortured cries echoed through the room and into the hallway. Then they were gone.

John rushed to Stephen.

"Are you okay?" he asked as he gave Stephen a hug.

"I think so."

"There is nothing to be afraid of. Nothing at all."

Belshazzon had put his swords back under his long jacket and faded into the corner of the room. John saw him and nodded at him acknowledging what he'd done.

"Try to get some sleep," John said.

John left the room, but he didn't go back to sleep. Instead, he headed to the library. There was something he needed to find inside the book. He knew there was another level to fighting the Gravine, but he'd never pursued it. He knew he should have. Things probably would have turned out differently if he had. He certainly wouldn't be at a loss to help Stephen now. Well, there was no time to look back and think "what if?" It was time to move forward. He wasn't losing this time.

John had a determination as he walked to the library. He was going to find out the answers they needed however long it took. After his grandfather left the room, Stephen closed his eyes and tried to go back to sleep. Just a few days ago, he knew nothing of Elyon, the

Enkeli, the Gravine or Gravinder. Life was relatively uncomplicated except for the kids at school who didn't like him, but they never tried to kill him. Stephen wondered what he'd gotten himself into. Stephen tried to sleep with his mind buzzing from the events of the past few days. Now another world was more real to him than the one he lived in. He was acutely aware that there was more to life than what he'd realized. Part of him wished he'd never seen into that dimension, but he was even more curious than ever.

He finally fell asleep. His mind continued to race in the dream state, where he saw himself and his grandfather traveling. He saw brief images as though someone was changing television channels without pausing on any of them to see what was on. They were blips across the screen of his subconscious mind. He saw images of Atlanta, Ga. He'd been to Atlanta before so he knew the golden-domed Georgia capitol building, the Olympic torch stand, the Georgia Aquarium and the Georgia Dome.

Then, he saw a montage of many faces, flashing before his eyes in a fast motion.

When he woke up the next morning, Stephen was exhausted. He looked at the clock beside his bed. He had slept until almost 10 a.m., but it was like he didn't sleep at all.

He pulled himself out of bed and went to search for his grandfather. As he walked out of his bedroom, he looked down the hallway, and he saw the library door was opened. His grandfather had been up since the wee hours of the morning reading and taking notes. Several pages were filled.

"Good morning, Stephen. Did you sleep?" John asked.

Stephen shook his head.

"I feel so tired this morning. It's like I went to sleep, but I wasn't asleep. I felt like I was going places."

John nodded.

"What exactly am I supposed to be doing?" Stephen asked. "I know that I'm some kind of keeper of the book, and that I'm supposed to help reunite Elyon's people. I just don't know what all of that means."

"Part of that we will have to find out together," said John. "I don't really know what it's all about either."

As they were talking, the doorbell rang.

John looked puzzled. People didn't visit their home. It was surrounded by woods on several acres of land, and the driveway wasn't easy to spot from the road. Making a trip there took an effort on the part of the visitor. People didn't just stumble upon it.

He almost didn't want to go to the door, but then the bell rang a second time.

He cautiously opened it, and he saw an elderly man standing outside. He had white hair and a white beard. He was wearing a dark overcoat and a hat, and he was carrying a cane.

"Hello John," said the visitor.

"Hello," he answered cautiously. He had no idea who this person was, and he wondered how he knew his name.

"The path is prepared for you and Stephen. You don't have to understand it. You don't have to know what is next. You don't have to know anything. You just have to trust. As you take one step, you will know what to do next. All will be revealed in time. Your part is just to follow the leading inside," he said and smiled. There was a twinkle in his eye.

John was aware that Stephen had walked up behind him. He turned for a split-second to look at Stephen.

"Sir, won't you come in?" John asked, but when he turned back, the man had vanished.

John stepped outside and looked around. All he saw were trees. There was no man, and there was no vehicle.

"Where did he go?" John asked Stephen. "Wasn't he here? I wasn't imaging this, was I?"

"No, I saw him too. He was definitely there."

"Remember that journal I told you about? This should go in there," said John. "He said we knew what to do."

As he turned to go back inside, John saw something on the

ground. He bent down and picked it up. It was a postcard of downtown Atlanta and underneath, there was a miniature key. He stared at it for a few minutes.

"What is it?" asked Stephen.

He reached out and took the postcard and key from his grandfather.

"Another key? I don't understand the first one yet. I had a dream about Atlanta last night. I saw different places there like some of the ones in this postcard. And I saw faces – lots and lots of faces," Stephen said.

"I had a dream about Atlanta, too," said John. "I guess we need to make a trip there."

"I wonder what's in Atlanta?" Stephen asked.

"I don't know, but it's like the man said – don't ask questions, just do what you know you are supposed to do," said John.

The two returned inside the house.

"Stephen, I want to give you something," said John as he paused in front of his bedroom door. He went into the room, which was filled with antique furnishings. He went over to the dresser, opened the top drawer and pulled out a box with a gold chain inside of it.

"I don't understand what the key is for, but I think you probably should keep it with you at all times," he said. "You can put it on this long chain and wear it. You can hide it under your shirt if you'd like. It's probably not something everyone needs to see. Or you can put it away in the box. For some reason, though, I think you should wear it for a while."

Stephen took the key out of his pocket and placed it on the chain. Then he put it around his neck.

The two headed toward the library.

"How are you doing after last night?" John asked.

"I'm okay," Stephen said and shrugged.

"You can't be afraid of them," John said. "If they know you're afraid of them, then they will have more power over you, and eventually, they will keep you from doing what you've been chosen to do. You have to keep your eyes focused on the overall goal. I am studying the book to learn more about what Elyon has provided for us. I know there are weapons to help us defeat the Gravine. Elyon defeated them in his realm, and the laws that apply in Elyon's realm apply to us here when fighting them. The Gravine may push the rules to their limits and beyond, but ultimately, there are higher powers that they have to submit to."

"Let these battles make you more determined to go after your goal," Stephen said. "Papa, are you sure we are supposed to be going places? You never want to leave the house unless you have to."

"Stephen, I messed up one time, and I tried to lock away my pain by closing myself off from the world. I can't do that anymore. I have been given a second chance. I won't fail this time," he said. "I have to overcome my fears and hurt."

6

The next morning John and Stephen loaded the pickup truck and headed on the road. The duo had gone on a few vacations, but usually, they involved the great outdoors. Taking a trip to into a city was a rarity. Stephen had been to Atlanta once as part of a field trip with his social studies' class.

He was excited to get away from the house because of the events of the past few days. The run-ins with the Gravine were emotionally and mentally draining. Atlanta was a few hours away so Stephen brought along some of the journals to read.

"Who was Samuel?" Stephen asked as he looked at the name in the front of one of the journal. It was more than a century old.

"Samuel was my grandfather. He was my dad's father," said John.

Stephen gently thumbed through the leather-bound book. The handwriting was bold, but it was ornate, making it a little difficult for the modern reader. Despite that, Stephen found himself drawn into Samuel's stories. He had great adventures, and he had a flair for telling them. Samuel often found himself visiting different locations. On these trips, he met many interesting people.

"Your grandfather sounded like a cool person. I wish I could have met him," said Stephen.

"I didn't really know him very well. I was about 10 when he died. My father was a few years younger than I am now when he became a father. My parents didn't think they would be able to have any children at all," said John. "And then, I was born. I remember bits and pieces of stories he and my father told. They were interesting."

Stephen read for a while longer.

"How long are we staying?" Stephen asked. "When your grandfather went places, he wasn't always there for a long time."

"We'll have to wait and see once we get there," he said. "What did you see in your dream?"

"I just saw the buildings in downtown," he said. "And then a lot of faces."

As Stephen was speaking, they spotted a billboard on the interstate. It had a key on it, and said *Find the key to your future*. It mentioned a store in downtown Atlanta.

"Well, I think we will head downtown," said John. "Did you see any fish in your dream? We could go to the aquarium."

"No fish, but that sounds good to me," Stephen said.

Stephen continued to read about Samuel's adventures. There were many times when Samuel would meet people who had forgotten they were Elyon's people; they'd forgotten he promised to protect them. When Samuel would talk to them and then talk about Elyon, it was like some long-buried memory was brought into their minds. Samuel turned on a light switch of sorts. They began to see what was there, but what had been hidden from them. Stephen realized he had to help people do that. They arrived in Atlanta with no incident. Their hotel was near the airport. After checking in, they took the train into downtown Atlanta.

Stephen and John weren't accustomed to being around so many people, but they were on a mission so they tried not to let the crowds bother them. They headed to the aquarium. John decided to use this opportunity to augment Stephen's homeschool science lessons while still looking for the reason they were there.

Lemachor and several other Gravine were following this expedition, studying their enemies' movements, trying to stay quietly in the background.

"Lemachor, what does all this mean?" asked Bestian.

"They are waking up Elyon's sleeping army," said Lemachor soberly. "Elyon is returning soon; our reign is drawing to a close. We will soon face our eternal punishment, and if we fail, we will face Gravinder's punishment as well."

He turned to look at Bestian.

"I'm not sure which of those is worse," Bestian said.

As Stephen and John walked through the aquarium, they had one eye on the exhibits and another for whatever it was they were supposed to find. After a couple of hours, they began to get tired.

"Do you think we should go somewhere else?" Stephen asked John.

"Let's stay just a little bit longer," he said. "I think we are in the right place."

Stephen was trying to juggle several things at one time. Not only did he have his computer notebook, but he also had a sketchpad and several pencils. With all of the colorful fish and other aquatic animals, there were plenty of things to sketch. He hadn't sketched anything yet so he decided to find a spot and sit. He wasn't really paying attention to where he was going and bumped into someone. He dropped his sketchpad and his pencils. The person he ran into also dropped some things.

"I'm sorry," said Stephen as he bent over to pick up his things. The key around his neck dangled in front of him. He looked up and saw a young girl. She had long red hair, freckles, and green eyes. She stopped and stared at the key.

"Where did you get that?" she asked and reached out as though she was going to grab it.

Stephen's first instinct was to hide it back in his shirt, but he then thought maybe this was the person he was here to meet.

"Someone very special gave it to me. Why?" he asked her.

She turned her head and then waved to someone. When she looked back at Stephen, she pulled out a chain, revealing a key exactly like the one Stephen was wearing. By this time, John had come over to see what was happening.

"I'm Lucy, and I'm 9," said the girl as she stuck out her hand to shake Stephen's. "You are a friend of Elyon so that means you can be my friend too."

"Hi, I'm Lucy's mom, Vanessa," said the woman Lucy had motioned to come near.

"I'm John, and this is my grandson, Stephen. It's nice to meet you," said John. He held out his hand and shook hers.

Their eyes met for a minute. She had the most beautiful green eyes John had ever seen. He found himself staring into them. Embarrassed, he broke the gaze hurriedly and looked away.

"Mama, look," Lucy said as she pointed to Stephen's key. "It's just like mine."

Vanessa reached out and lightly touched Stephen's key.

"That's not possible, Lucy," Vanessa's voice caught in her throat as she spoke. She shook her head as she stared at Stephen's key.

"It is possible. I told you this was real. I told you I wasn't imaging things. Stop taking me to that doctor. He doesn't know anything," she said.

John and Stephen looked at each other.

"Papa, I'm hungry. Let's get something to eat, and maybe Lucy and her mom could join us?" Stephen asked.

"I'm hungry too, Mama. Let's go," said Lucy grabbing her mother by the hand.

Vanessa looked at John. She thought it would probably be safe since he had a child with him, and they were heading to another public place. They found a restaurant nearby in downtown Atlanta. Stephen and Lucy began to excitedly share their stories with each other even before they got a table, often interrupting the other because their stories had many similarities They seemed oblivious to everyone around them including John and Vanessa.

Lucy's family also had a book that had been in her family for many years. It had been locked away in a chest in the attic of her grandparents' home. Her grandmother had died a few weeks before. Lucy and her mom had lived with her grandmother for a couple of months. One day, Lucy went upstairs to see if she could find anything interesting. She saw the chest and thought it might have some kind of treasure inside of it. It was curious because she saw shimmering light coming through the box. When she opened it, all she found was a book, but the book was illuminated. She took it out and placed it on the floor of the attic. It grew larger. She opened it up and fell into it just like Stephen had.

As they talked to each other, the phrases "Me too!" "Omigosh," and "I can't believe this," were interjected frequently into the conversation.

"I told you I wasn't crazy Mom," Lucy said. "But you didn't believe. Now that doctor thinks I'm crazy. You know you should listen to me."

Lucy had a brassy and bold personality. She wasn't a pushover, and she spoke her mind in spite of the fact that it often got her into trouble. She seemed much older than her nine years on the planet.

"You don't know how hard it was to get her to bring me here today," Lucy said to Stephen and John. "She didn't want to listen to me, but I knew that something would happen if we came."

"You're right, Lucy," said a stunned Vanessa. "I thought Elyon was an imaginary friend, and I had no idea where she got the key."

"So, you didn't know about the book in your family?" John asked Vanessa.

"Well, I'd heard about it, but my mother was very quiet. My father wouldn't listen to her. He was pretty mean about it actually. He forbade her to talk about it around us. I know she cried a lot when he wasn't around. When Lucy had this happen to her, I thought it was insane talk, but she wouldn't stop. Then all these things started happening in the house. Lucy woke up with unexplained cuts and bruises. She would talk about the wild dreams she had. She showed me that key, and she told me that some alien or something had given it to her. I took her to a psychiatrist who said she was having problems dealing with her grief. These dreams and imaginations were her way of coping," Vanessa replied. "The doctor said she was probably cutting herself as well."

"That is so not true. That doctor is so wrong," said Lucy. "I didn't make any of this up, and why would I cut myself? That's just dumb."

"Have you experienced anything?" John asked.

"No, I don't think so. Well, I don't really know. My mother had cancer, but she responded well to treatment. Then, it came back in her liver. Initially, I was going to take a few weeks off from work to help her. She began to deteriorate rapidly. It spread so fast. She went from being a vibrant woman to dying within three months. I ended up quitting my job because I couldn't leave my mother. My father died about a year before my mother. He was killed in a car accident," Vanessa explained. "I was so consumed with making sure my mother was comfortable that I lost sight of a lot of things. I wasn't thinking clearly, and then when my mother died, I was overwhelmed."

"Did Lucy find the book before your mother died?" John asked.

"Yes," said Lucy. "I did."

Vanessa raised an eyebrow.

"Really?" Vanessa asked.

"I didn't know what to tell you because you didn't believe me," said Lucy. "I found the book about a week before she died. It was cool because it glowed. Somehow, I knew not to ask you about it so I took it to Nana one day when you had gone to the grocery store. She told me about Elyon, and how the book could take me to meet him. She smiled when she thought about Elyon. She seemed very happy and not in pain. It was like he was her friend. She told me she was sorry that she had not taught you about Elyon. When I told her I had already met Elyon, it really made her happy. The night Nana died, I went into her room after you'd gone to sleep, and I took the book with me. She had asked me to bring it to her so I did. She went with me to see Elyon. She didn't have cancer over there, and she didn't have gray hair or any pain. She laughed, and she was so happy. Elyon was happy to see her. They knew each other. Before we came back here, Nana told me she wanted to be free. She told me not to be sad because she wasn't going to hurt any more. She would look the way

I had seen her that night. Then she said that we would be together again one day, and we could dance and sing."

Tears rolled down Vanessa's face as she listened to Lucy's story.

"I wanted to tell you all of that, but you didn't believe me," Lucy said.

Vanessa hugged Lucy and continued to cry for a few more minutes.

"I'm sorry, baby. I'm sorry I didn't believe you," she said.

Vanessa looked at John. She hadn't thought of any men as being attractive since before she met her late husband, Charlie, and that was such a long time ago. She wondered how on earth was she attracted to this man she just met.

"My mother has only been gone for about three weeks," said Vanessa. "Lucy's all I have now. I don't know what to make of this with Lucy and Elyon."

"I know it's a lot to take in for now. Do you live in Atlanta?" John asked.

"No, we lived in Nashville, Tenn., and my mother lives - lived - near Gatlinburg, " she replied. "I was going through some of my mother's things, and I found some pictures of Lucy and my mother from a few years ago. They were taken at the aquarium. When Lucy saw them, she insisted we go today. We have to get back on the road before it's too late. This was obviously no accident that we met you here today."

"It's definitely no accident," John said and nodded. "Before you go, could I ask Lucy one more question?"

"Of course," said Vanessa.

"Lucy, did Elyon tell you anything about your key?" John asked.

Lucy thought for a moment.

"He said I would know how to use it when I needed it and not to worry about it until then," said Lucy.

John and Stephen walked Lucy and Vanessa back to the parking garage and said their goodbyes. John and Vanessa exchanged cell numbers and email addresses.

"Thank you. I have some things I'd like to ask you," she said.

The two of them made their way to the train station.

"So, then there are other people who are also keepers of the book, not just us?" Stephen asked.

"Yes, Stephen. Elyon has met with human beings for centuries, and he has given copies of the Book of Ancient Wisdom to help them while they live on earth. It's even more important now as he prepares to return and set up his kingdom. His people have to know how to fight the Gravine. We will play an important role in his return. I believe there is something special about you and your role, but the job is bigger than one person can handle," he said. "You will need to help others, and others will have to help you. You don't want to be alone in this."

"It's a relief to know that. It scared me to think that it was going to be me. I'm just a kid."

"It's going to take a lot of us. Elyon's people are scattered all over the planet. There's no way for you to get to millions of people. It will take some help," John said.

"I like Lucy. I'd like to be friends with her."

"I think we'll see more of Lucy and her mother. They have lots of questions. I think we accomplished everything we were supposed to accomplish. We need to head home tonight as well."

"Okay. Do you think we'll be going a lot of places?"

"Yes. I think this is the start of something," John replied.

7

Stephen was tired from the trip and climbed into bed as soon as they arrived home. It wasn't long before he was asleep, and the nightmares returned. In this one, it was dark, and he was running. He was outside this time, and it was cold. He knew he was being chased, but he didn't know who or what was chasing him. He was out of breath and realized he was at the edge of a cliff. He turned around and stumbled. Something reached out and grabbed his ankles. He remembered the sharp claws of the Gravine in his ankles. There seemed like more than one set of claws. It was very painful. Stephen began screaming as they pulled him closer to the edge of the cliff. He tried to claw at the ground, but there was nothing for him to hold onto, nothing to stop him from being dragged away.

He looked up and saw many of the Gravine hissing at him. He was afraid. He looked down at his ankles and saw two Gravine dragging him, one at each leg. Their talons were sharper than the others. He looked back and saw his grandfather. He looked like a soldier. He was wearing some type of high tech body armor. The Gravine didn't even seem to know he was walking through them. The armor seemed to shield him from them. He burst toward Stephen and grabbed his arms.

John was in the library, but he could hear screams coming from Stephen's room. He rushed down the hallway and burst into the room, where he saw his grandson thrashing and kicking on the bed.

There were no other beings in the room except Belshazzon who was on alert. John grabbed Stephen's shoulders and shook him.

"Stephen," he said in a firm voice.

Stephen woke with a start. He was out of breath as though he'd run a long distance. He looked down at his ankles, and there was nothing there. This had been a dream?

"What's wrong?" John asked.

"The Gravine. They were coming after me, and they wanted to drag me over the side of a cliff. It was awful," he said.

"It's okay now," said John.

"You were in the dream. You came to rescue me, and you were dressed like a soldier with this really cool armor. It protected you from the Gravine and made you invisible for a few minutes. They didn't know you were coming."

"Armor. I've been studying in the book about some armor. I think we need to figure out how to use it and start. We need all the help we can get. We'll check it out in the morning."

John sat there for a few minutes. It was late so he decided to go to bed, but he tossed and turned for a few hours. He got up before dawn. As he left his room and headed toward the library, he could see the book. It had expanded again, and shafts of light flooded the hallway. He'd never seen it like that. He felt a lump in his throat. This was something he'd only dreamed about. While he was happy for Stephen's experience, he had felt a mix of jealousy and regret when he listened to Stephen's story. He knew that he should have been able to share his experiences with his grandson, but he had none. Now, it was going to be his turn. He slowly walked down the hallway. He hesitated and took a deep breath when he got to the library door . He walked toward the book, and as he got closer, he reached out to touch it. The action opened the portal, and he fell into the book.

It was as Stephen had said and what had been written in the journals but better. This time it was his turn. The colors of the portal were brighter and crisper than any colors he'd ever seen on Earth. All of his cares began to melt away as he flew higher. Not only did the cares leave, but the sense of regret and sadness, the remnants of grief and depression still deeply embedded in him completely left. He felt like singing to the beautiful music he heard as he floated. The reds, blues, and greens wrapped around him like ribbons as he journeyed.

When he arrived at the Jeweled City, he was surprised he wasn't blinded by the brightness of the city. As he entered the city, he saw many of the beings Stephen had described. He was approached by a large man with dark skin. He wore a long flowing white robe and had jet black hair.

"Elyon is expecting you. I am Melzurek," he said. "I will be escorting you. Elyon has some things he wants you to see while you are here."

John felt that familiar lump rise back into his throat. He was finally going to meet Elyon face to face. The apprehension tried to fill his mind again. This was long overdue; he should have been here years ago. He felt a fleeting sense of shame that he hadn't responded when he was first called. They walked down a long corridor. The walls were opaque like pearl and encrusted with jewels. John noticed the white robes of his escort shimmered in the light as he moved. He didn't seem to be walking as John was; rather, he seemed to float across the floor. John saw Elyon's throne room ahead of him. He wondered what he would say? All sorts of apologies ran through John's head. They all sounded weak. Melzurek led him into a magnificent room, and at the top of a high set of stairs, Elyon was seated upon his throne. John got closer, fell to his knees, and bowed his head.

Elyon motioned for him to come to the platform at the top of the staircase. Stunned, John looked at Melzurek who nodded reassuring him. John kept his eyes on each milky white stair, which sparkled with an array of jewels; there were rubies, emeralds, sapphires, amethysts, and opals. When he reached the top step, he fell to his knees once more.

"I'm so sorry I didn't respond to you years ago. I'm sorry I let my anger and fear get the best of me. I'm sorry." The words fell out of John's mouth before Elyon stopped him.

"There's nothing to apologize for," Elyon said.

At that point, John looked up and into his eyes. There was no malice in his face; he wasn't mocking John. He was genuine in what he said.

"I'll never force anyone to do anything. The choice is always up to you. There is plenty of time for you to fulfill what you need to fulfill. Time means nothing to me, and I have the ability to alter it. It's only too late after you've died. You have plenty of life left in you, John. Don't you feel how you've been rejuvenated over the past few weeks?" Elyon asked and smiled.

John nodded.

"I should've started sooner," said John.

"You cannot go through life with regret. Although you feel you've missed out on things in life, everything you've gone through has prepared you for the place you are in now. The best is still ahead of you. The next few years will be very busy, and there are many surprises in store for you; just enjoy the journey along the way."

"I don't feel I'm prepared to help Stephen. There are things I still don't know."

"Stephen isn't the only one with a task. You play a vital role as well. As you continue to look for answers, you will find them. Listen to me in the whispers of your thoughts. You must go many places, and time is running out," Elyon said.

"Yes, I will do what I need to do."

"Stephen had a dream about you in armor. You have had several encounters with the Gravine. As you continue on your journey, they will continue their fight against you. And it will become more intense. They know their time is running short. If you will use the armor and be mindful of its purpose, you will be able to withstand their onslaught," Elyon said.

He motioned to Melzurek who had several items draped across his outstretched arms. All of the pieces contained that illuminated quality.

"You will know you are wearing these items. The Gravine will know you are wearing these items, but not everyone else will. As far as others are concerned, they will be invisible. This is a belt of truth. Things won't always be what they seem. You will only know what is true when you are wearing this," he said.

John took the golden belt and placed it around his waist. It didn't weigh a lot, but when he put it on, he was aware of its presence.

Elyon then took a vest.

John took it and looked at it. It resembled chain mail, but it was not made of metal. Instead, it was a strong fiber mesh; the threads were strands of light.

"This vest covers your heart. The heart has long been a symbol in your world for the place of emotions. It will help you act rightly and justly toward people. People aren't always going to want to hear what you have to say. You will know what to do when you wear this," Elyon said.

Next, there was a pair of boots.

"I haven't called you to go to war with people. Your battle isn't with other human beings. There are some who have chosen to follow after the way of Gravinder. He has power in your world, and he seduces people with the possibilities of it. These shoes will remind you that you are to walk in peace."

Then there was a helmet.

"You need to keep your thoughts in line; stay on target; focus on what you know."

And lastly, there was a sword and a shield.

The sword had a double-edge, and it was inscribed as well.

The book is a light for your feet.

Like everything else, the sword was illuminated.

"This sword connects with the life force inside the Book of Ancient wisdom. It also connects with the words you say. It will help you damage the enemy, but you must learn how to use it properly. I have some other things I want to show you. You must return home first and learn to use these gifts."

He smiled at John.

"There are good times ahead of you. I can guarantee it," he said.
"Thank you," John replied.

John was back in the library. He looked down. He couldn't see the armor, but he could sense that it was there. He glanced next to him, and on the floor in a neat pile, were the same items Elyon had given to him but for Stephen.

When Stephen woke up, John helped him with his armor. As they read more in the book, the discovered the armor wasn't some type of magical equipment, but it required mental discipline on the part of the wearer to be functional, especially when it came to using the shield and the sword.

8

John soon discovered Stephen was not his only student. Lucy and Stephen's encounter with Elyon had come within days of each other. And it was no coincidence for the four of them to meet on that dreary January day in Atlanta. At least, John had a frame of reference to help Stephen, and he had many volumes of journals as well as a brief knowledge of the book. Vanessa had nothing to base Lucy's experience on. Had she not met John and Stephen she would have spent a lot of time convinced her daughter was crazy and not understanding her purpose.

While he wanted to help them, he also had an attraction to Vanessa, and that was disturbing to him. He didn't have many friends and certainly no female ones. He was an attractive man, but he had shut himself down emotionally after Meredith left. He didn't want that pain again so he built up many walls. When Aaron left, he felt a different kind of rejection – that, in many ways, was worse than what Meredith had caused. And now that he finally had a purpose for his life, he didn't want anything to distract him from what he knew he was supposed to be doing.

About a week after they met, Vanessa called John.

"Hi, John. This is Vanessa. Is this a bad time for you?" she asked. She sounded a little unnerved.

"Hello. No. No. This is fine. Is everything okay?" he asked.

"Well. Lucy has been having these nightmares the past few

nights. She tells me about these horrible looking creatures chasing her. They have claws and fangs. And they want her key," she said.

"Those are the Gravine," John replied. He spent the next hour on the phone instructing Vanessa on how to fight them and reassuring her that Lucy would be all right.

"This is so overwhelming," she said. "The next thing I'm going to ask you may seem a little crazy. I hardly know you, but in a way, I feel like I've known you all of my life. I need to go through some more of my mother's things so I can sell the house. I'm sure there are things there that are clues to her past and to Lucy's future. I don't want to overlook any of them. Is there any way you and Stephen could come and help us?"

"I think that could be arranged. I meant to ask you this before, but what about your husband?"

"My husband died when Lucy was about 3 years-old. He had cancer," she said, her voice cracking.

"I'm sorry to hear that."

"What about you? I guess I should have asked if you had a wife before I asked if you could come and help me. I wasn't thinking. I apologize."

"Oh. I have been divorced for many, many years. Stephen is actually my grandson. Stephen's father was just a baby when my wife left. I never saw her again. The last time I heard from her was when the divorce papers showed up, and then Stephen's parents died when he was just a few months old. He's lived with me ever since."

John and Vanessa continued to talk for several more hours.

Vanessa was only a few years younger than John. Their stories were quite different. Vanessa had a career she loved, and she didn't meet her husband, Charlie, until she was in her late 30s. They had a whirlwind courtship and married only a few weeks after their initial meeting. Lucy came almost on their first anniversary. They were talking about having another child soon after, but plans changed when he was diagnosed with lung cancer.

Charlie responded well to treatment, and doctors couldn't find

a trace of cancer. Then on Lucy's third birthday, Charlie started
coughing up blood. They rushed him to the emergency room and
found that not only had the cancer returned, but it had spread. He
was dead within two months. Watching her mother go through a
similar path brought up many hard memories for Vanessa. Charlie
worked at a bank, and he had carefully invested in some real estate.
Those investments provided for Vanessa so she didn't have to work
after he died. She decided to go back to work because she enjoyed
meeting people and getting out of the house. Since her mother's
death, she was having problems with grief and depression. She and
her mother were close, but her mother never talked about the life
Lucy was starting to lead. It saddened her more to know her father's
abuse of her mother had prevented her from knowing a huge part
of her mother's life. Talking to John was comforting for her. She felt
she'd known him for years even though they'd just met.

John thought the same thing as he hung up the phone, and he
thought about Elyon's words to him – that there were good things
ahead for him. He was surprised at how quickly the time passed as
he spoke to Vanessa that evening. For the first time in many years,
he didn't feel pain. He didn't fear rejection; he didn't fear anything.
He felt free from much of the baggage he'd carried for all those years.
There was something about his meeting with Elyon. He left Jeweled
City a different man. Maybe this would be another second chance.
He was getting the second chance to fulfill his destiny; was there a
second chance at love for him too?

Lemachor also saw this as a second chance. He was looking for
an inroad. Since Stephen's journey through the book, things had not
gone well for Lemachor and his forces. This could be an opportunity
to get John's eyes off of what he'd started with Stephen and onto other
things. It had worked before when John met Meredith. Lemachor
couldn't wait to try it again. Distractions were powerful. If they get
too close, then he can unleash distrust and confusion into the mix.
Rejection and heartbreak were the ways to get John off target.

"The power of suggestion to the weak-minded is all too easy," said

Lemachor to Bestian as they plotted their course. "Let's have some fun, shall we?"

John began making reservations for a hotel. There was one not too far from Vanessa's mother's home.

While John was on the phone, Stephen wrote more in his journal. He wrote about putting on the armor that his grandfather had received on his trip into the Jeweled City. Stephen wanted to go back there. He wanted to know what else was available to him on his journey. He was also interested in this armor. He had the opportunity to test it out that evening. He knew that his grandfather was on the phone with Vanessa, and for such a long time too. Usually, he and John spent the evenings together. They liked to play video games together, and sometimes, they'd watch television. Since Stephen didn't have any siblings or parents and they lived so far away from other people, John was it. He was the only companion Stephen had, and he really enjoyed the time he spent with him. This long conversation with Vanessa bothered him. She was taking time away from him.

She should figure this out for herself, Stephen thought. *She has a book too. She can read it.*

Stephen found himself getting agitated. He paced the hallway outside the living room where his grandfather was talking. He went up to John a few times trying to get his attention. Each time, John held up his hand as if to say *not now.* That just made Stephen angry. Finally, he sulked to his room, and he looked for a book to read. He liked superheroes and adventure stories. As he looked over his shelves to find something he hadn't read recently, he had a thought about the armor. A piece of the armor was a helmet, and part of the purpose of the helmet was to protect the mind. Also, the vest which protected his chest and symbolized guarding his emotions. Out of control thoughts and emotions can lead to unwise choices.

Getting mad at his grandfather would accomplish nothing, and he did like Lucy as a friend. John was trying to help Vanessa understand some things. Stephen didn't want people thinking Lucy was crazy because he knew she wasn't.

That's all part of the mission, Stephen thought. He is supposed to tell Elyon's people about his coming, and he is supposed to help people by gathering them to Elyon. Pushing people away isn't part of it. Vanessa and Lucy need their help.

He was also reminded of something else that he'd read in the book. It said he had to control his thoughts. If they were contrary to what the mission was and if they were contrary to what the book said, then he needed to return his focus to what was important. The book talked a lot about controlling your thoughts and actions. Thoughts lead to actions, and actions have consequences.

That was something else to write in his journal. While all the cool experiences were good to write about, there was something else to write about the practical life lessons he was daily coming to grips with.

He found one of his adventure books and starting reading it. It wasn't as interesting as his real life so he put it away. He was just about to go to bed when he heard a knock on the door.

"Hi," John opened the door and stuck his head in.

"Come in," said Stephen.

"I'm sorry I was on the phone with Vanessa for so long. She had a lot of questions."

"I heard. I had the chance to learn a little more about the helmet and chest protector vest. I'm not sure I like this. It's going to be really hard. I realized I couldn't be mad at her or you even though I really wanted to be. I know we have to help them. I just like having time with you. You are my friend."

"You are my friend too, and you will always be my friend. Don't ever forget that," John said.

He gave Stephen a hug.

"There is one other thing," John continued. "Vanessa has asked us to come and visit for a couple of days. She is cleaning out her mother's house, and she wants us to come help her look through her things to see if there is anything that we think would be a clue as to her mother's life. She thinks her mother had been trying to tell her things all her life. She feels bad for having missed out on the things her mother was trying to say. She also thinks she may not have really known her mother. She's having a rough time."

Stephen nodded.

"She lives near Gatlinburg, Tenn. There's white water rafting nearby," he said with a smile.

"Yea, but the water is still; it's not spring yet," said Stephen.

"Nothing like white water rafting in the cold."

"Maybe we could go fishing or something while we're there. At least, there won't be any snakes."

"Yep. It's too cold for snakes," John said. "We'll just be gone for a couple of days."

9

Vanessa really wasn't sure what they would be looking for among her mother's belongings. There seemed to be a huge gap in the person she thought she knew and the person her mother really was. Had she missed something along the way? She tried to think about the conversations they had toward the end of her life. She went over every word she could remember. Looking back, there were hints of things. Maybe what Vanessa had dismissed as the babblings of a woman taking too many painkillers had actually been more.

Elyon. Had my mother said that name before? she wondered.

There was a knock at the door. She heard Lucy's voice.

"Mama, they're here," Lucy called out.

Vanessa walked to the front door to greet her guests.

"Thank you for coming. Lucy and I have put together a lot of questions we have for you."

"There's plenty of time for that," said John.

"Let me show you around. I don't really know if there's anything here that might be important. I know she must have been communicating to me about Elyon. She must have been trying to tell us something, but I missed all the hints. I guess I thought she had dementia as well as cancer. I don't know," said Vanessa.

"It's okay."

They passed through the front parlor into a living room with a fireplace.

John heard Stephen gasp, and immediately, he saw the reason. On one of the shelves in the living room was a shadow box with several old-fashioned skeleton keys.

"What's the matter?" asked Vanessa.

John walked over to the box and pulled it from the shelf.

While there were several keys in there, only one really stood out. There were seven keys in the box; they seemed to be set in a decorative pattern. They were different sizes; some were simple; some ornate. All were lackluster except for one. It shone like it had just been polished despite the fact that the glass on the box was covered with a layer of dust.

"How did you see that, Stephen?" John asked him.

"I saw light reflecting off of it."

Vanessa took the box and lifted off the glass.

"It looks just like Lucy's," she said, and she began to cry. "It's been here all the time. I remember seeing this years ago."

John had never seen a key before Stephen had shown him his. Were there keys hidden in the house somewhere, and he didn't know about them? Did this key fit to a specific door?

"Now, you can have one too, Mom," said Lucy.

Vanessa turned to Stephen.

"Thank you," Vanessa said. "I knew that by bringing you here I'd find something."

All of a sudden John felt inadequate. He should have been the one with the knowledge. After all, his family had been a keeper of the book for many generations. While he did have some things passed down to him, he realized there was a lot he'd missed.

Vanessa had taken the key out of the box and looked at it.

"What does it say?" Lucy asked her excitedly.

"It says 'only believe,'" Vanessa answered.

Lucy smiled.

"See, I told you if you would believe that Stephen and John would help us, then we would find things in Nana's house," said Lucy.

"John, do you have a key?" asked Vanessa.

John looked a little sad.

"No," he said softly. "I don't have a key."

Vanessa looked a little embarrassed that she had asked the question. She didn't like that it made John uncomfortable.

"Why don't we have something to eat? And then, we can take a look in the attic," she said trying to fill the awkward silence.

Stephen felt badly for his grandfather. Since Stephen went into the book, he hadn't seen his grandfather sad. Now that old familiar look was back upon his face. He'd liked the changes that had come over him in recent days. He didn't want his grandfather to go back to what he had been before. He touched his arm.

"If there are keys at home, we will find them," Stephen said.

John nodded and smiled.

The next two days were a blur of looking through neatly arranged boxes in the attic. They started looking in the box where Lucy found the book, but there was nothing else in the chest containing it. There were multitudes of boxes filled with old love letters, Vanessa's report cards and school papers and tons of photographs. Vanessa's mother didn't throw anything away, but she kept things meticulously organized. They spent hours shredding documents and bills from decades before. They threw away a lot of things.

Vanessa decided to abandon the search in the attic.

"Maybe we should look somewhere else," she said to John. The two of them hadn't realized that Lucy and Stephen had left the room hours ago.

"I wonder if they've found anything," John said.

They walked through all of the rooms in the house and didn't see the two of them.

"I wonder where they could be," said Vanessa, who sounded a little afraid.

"Lucy," she called. "Lucy."

They walked back upstairs to her mother's bedroom and noticed a light coming from the closet door. Vanessa opened the closet, but all she saw at first was clothes. Lucy appeared through the clothing. She seemed excited.

"Mama, you have got to come see this," said Lucy as she dragged her mother through to the other side of the clothes.

There was a panel in the back of the closet, leading to a secret room. It wasn't a large room, but this was what they were looking for. Inside were numerous paintings of Elyon, the Enkeli and the Jeweled City. There were pen and ink and charcoal drawings. She also had some mixed media and collages. There was one painted with a blue acrylic background with a silver, glitter covered cube in the center. Pasted onto the canvas were cutouts of golden keys. They were all hung neatly in rows. It was obvious they had not been painted in the room as there was no ventilation. There were no art supplies. It was simply a gallery. Also, in the room was a small bookcase with several notebooks and leather bound books.

Vanessa slowly walked into the room.

"I had no idea this was here," Vanessa said. "Not long before my mother died, she directed me to the closet. I thought she wanted a sweater. She was so weak. She couldn't really speak much. It took too much effort. She was irritated when I couldn't bring her what she wanted from the closet."

She looked at Lucy.

"How did you find this room?" Vanessa asked.

"Well, we got bored looking through all those papers," said Lucy. "So Stephen and I decided to explore. When we walked downstairs, we saw light coming from Nana's room, but there wasn't a light on."

"The light was coming from underneath the closet door," said Stephen. "We opened the door and started to look for the light because the clothes were blocking it. When we moved the clothes out of the way, we found this room."

"Look, Mom. There are no lights in here, but we can see," said Lucy.

Vanessa and John stood in the middle of the room speechless. There were no windows in the room yet the room was filled with a warm light. Vanessa walked up to one of the paintings. She saw on the bottom right corner the signature – Emily Shaw. Vanessa began to cry.

"I never knew my mother could paint," Vanessa said through the tears. "She was so talented."

John put his hand on Vanessa's arm.

"Stephen and I are going to go now," he said. "We will leave you and Lucy alone."

"Thank you. Thank you so much," she said and turned to give him a hug.

When she placed her head on his chest, she began to weep harder. John held her for a few minutes. She lifted her head and stepped back. She felt awkward that she had been weeping in the arms of someone she hadn't known very long.

"I'm sorry," she said as she wiped tears away.

"It's okay," said John, and he motioned to Stephen it was time to leave.

"Bye, Lucy," said Stephen.

After they left, they decided to go to a restaurant to get something to eat.

Stephen could tell something was bothering John. He wondered if it had to do with the key. Stephen knew what it was like to feel left out of something. So he tried to think of something to say that would get his mind off of it.

"Those paintings were amazing," said Stephen. "They were like the paintings I saw when you took me to the museum."

"I didn't really get a good look at them. Maybe, I will get a chance to one day," John said.

"There was something special about that room. I felt the same way there that I did when I went to the Jeweled City. Nothing bothered me. I just wanted to sit there for a while even though there was nothing to do in there. It was really cool."

John nodded.

"I think we accomplished what we were supposed to accomplish here. You're right about it being too cold for whitewater rafting. Let's see if we can rent a boat while we are here and go fishing – just you and me," John said.

"That sounds like fun."

The next morning they headed on their fishing trip. Stephen tried to make small talk with his grandfather, but he was not responding with more than "yes" or "no" answers. He could tell his grandfather's thoughts were far away from their fishing boat. He almost said something about what he'd learned with the armor, but then he decided not to. The brooding grandfather was the one he'd always known. Sure, there were glimpses of a fun and adventurous person. While he loved his grandfather, he certainly was having more fun with the other person he'd seen in the past few weeks. After a couple of hours of no talking and no catching anything, Stephen was ready to go home.

"Can we leave now?" Stephen asked.

John looked relieved.

"Papa, we will find your key."

John looked away quickly, but Stephen thought he saw a tear.

"It's going to be just fine, Papa," he said.

"Stephen, sometimes, you are wise beyond your years."

10

The ride home went by fast.

"Do you think there are any hidden rooms in our home?" Stephen asked before they reached the house. "I mean it's a pretty big place."

"You know, I've often wondered if there were any hidden rooms," he said. "I think we have an adventure in front of us."

Stephen noticed the sadness leaving his grandfather's face, and it made him smile.

Once they had arrived, John was ready to find out what other mysteries there were. The family home was about 200 years old. It had been passed down from generation-to-generation. The original structure was a simple farmhouse; over the years, more rooms had been added. The lower level of the home held the library, living room, the kitchen, bathrooms, and two bedrooms. The two bedrooms were not originally bedrooms. The upper floor had four bedrooms, and there was an attic. John wasn't sure how long it had been since anyone lived upstairs. On the grounds, there was his workshop, which was separate from the home, and there was a small guest cottage. The key could be almost anywhere – if there was one.

Before he ventured to the upstairs rooms, he wanted to see if there was anything he'd overlooked in the library. In the past few weeks, he and Stephen had spent a lot of time in there, but he wasn't looking for a key.

"Let's check the library first," John said.

"Aren't we going to unpack?"

"You can if you want."

John placed his bag on the floor and headed straight to the library. He didn't know where to search first. Over the next several hours, he pulled out every journal and thumbed through the pages. He had to be careful because most of the books were more than a century old. Stephen helped too, but he got tired after several hours. He walked back to his room and went to bed. He didn't even think his grandfather noticed when he left the room. John was intent on his mission. He hadn't realized how many books were in the room. He wasn't even reading them, but he did notice simple drawings of keys in one or two of them. He'd never seen them before. There was no explanation of what the keys symbolized or if they had a practical purpose. He pulled out the books hoping to trip a switch that led to a secret passageway just like in old movies, but he didn't find any. He looked behind furniture to see if there were hidden drawers or latches that led somewhere. He looked inside one of the desk drawers and found something he hadn't seen in about 30 years.

He recognized the handwriting on the front of the envelope immediately. It was the letter Meredith had written to him when she left. He felt a stab of pain as he opened the letter. The writing was smudged and the paper warped from the tears he cried onto it many years before. The letter explained that she had never really been in love with him, but she only married him because she wanted to make an old boyfriend jealous. He was the true love of her life. It had all been a mistake. Her old boyfriend had found her and been calling. She wanted to be with him. She explained she couldn't be a good mother, but she knew that he would make a good father. She said she was sorry that he loved her the way he did. She knew he loved her, but his love for her wasn't enough. It wasn't a long letter, but it was all she left.

Those words had been like daggers to the heart for many years. He thought they'd cause the same response as they had in the past, but no tears came. There were none left to cry. He closed his eyes and thought about the way his attitudes had changed lately. He was ready to let go of Meredith and let go of the past with all its hurts.

He looked around and realized Stephen had left the room. John thought Stephen probably had the right idea. He decided to give up on the search and go to bed.

There were no nightmares for Stephen, just a restful sleep, but on the other side of the hallway, his grandfather was having a different type of dream. He had come to terms with some things of his past, but the lack of the key revealed there was a deeper struggle inside. While his heart and emotions had been healed of many of his past hurts, there were still sore spots, and these spots were places he could be exploited.

In his dream, he saw hundreds of people each with a key, but they had physical wounds. Some had broken arms; some had horrible diseases; and some had gashes and abrasions visible on their bodies. As he walked past each one, he held out his hand. He stopped and smiled. He told them Elyon had sent him, and instantly, their wounds were healed. They were excited their pain and suffering was gone. He touched many of them. As soon as they were healed, they vanished. At the end of the dream, he stood alone in front of Elyon.

"It's not the gifts that make you special, John," Elyon said. "There are a lot of gifted people. It's not the gifts that make me accept you . Don't be defined by the gifts. Know that you are special because of who you are, not what you do. Don't look at what you lack. I need everyone working together."

John woke up. With a key or without one, John still had a vital part to play. Even if he didn't have all the answers he thought he should have, it was going to be okay. He took a deep breath. It seemed his own healing was taking more time than those he saw in the dream, but with each encounter with Elyon, he could shed more of his emotional weights.

When will they all be gone? he thought.

John didn't sleep much that night. He got up early, and he

kept thinking about the dream. He went to the book. In it, he read something very simple. Each person has a role to play; each person has different gifts and abilities. Not everyone was made the same.

I guess it's time to move on and really let the past be in the past. There are second chances. What's next? John thought.

In the background, Lemachor was pacing. He'd been throwing self doubt, regret, and rejection up to John a lot lately. And while they initially worked, John seemed to be shaking them off. What was the problem? They always worked in the past. He didn't like that he was losing his touch. It was time for another strategy.

Stephen got up the next morning expecting to find his grandfather still furiously tearing through the library or possibly upstairs searching for the key. Instead, he found him at the computer.

"Did you find a key?" Stephen asked.

"No, but I realized that was not what was important. It's not the key that gives me my purpose or proves to me that I am needed in this mission. It was getting me off of the focus. Our mission is to help gather Elyon's scattered people and help them in their fight against the Gravine. And we have to continue on our progress of learning how to fight them and move forward," John said. "I've actually gotten a few emails from people asking us to come and help them prepare for their fight."

"How did they find your email address, and how can we help them?"

"That I'm not sure about. It's like the old gentleman who showed up at our house and knew my name. I'm going to write a few of them back and see what I can find out. I guess we will help them the same way we've helped Vanessa and Lucy. We just share with them what we know, and we point to the book for the rest of the answers. Sometimes, our experiences will help them as well."

"I know that I've had a couple of experiences with the Gravine, but are they really out there waiting to get us? I mean, it's a little hard to believe. They aren't bothering us right now."

"They always come back. There might be time in between what

they do, but they are always plotting and waiting for an opportunity. If we get lax and aren't expecting them, then they could get a victory. It's standard warfare to try and catch your opponent when no one is expecting you. Sneak attacks are often very successful. That's why we have to be on guard all the time because it's not a question of if, but when."

"I guess so."

"But think about what we've learned over the past few weeks. We've received keys in other ways. Maybe not a key like you have, but key principles that will work. Also, we now have some protective gear. I think we have to share that with people," John said.

"I have had dreams lately about us traveling and going to different countries. This is going to take a lot of time."

"I don't know how long it will take."

"Have you talked to Vanessa?"

"No. I probably should see how they are doing," John said. "I think I'll do that now."

John moved away from the computer, but he left his email open. Stephen sat down and looked at the screen. The subject lines of the emails reflected requests from all over the world. There were emails from Thailand, Greece, Australia and New Zealand. Some were written in languages he couldn't understand.

"I guess we won't go there," Stephen said as he looked one with Greek letters.

John hoped Vanessa wasn't upset with him. It had been a couple of days since he spoke to her, and he didn't tell her specifically they were leaving. When she asked for time to absorb things, he didn't want to pry, and he wanted to give her some space. He wondered if two days was long enough.

He called her cell phone, and it went straight to voice mail.

"Hi, Vanessa. It's John. Stephen and I came home yesterday. We wanted to give you the space you needed. Please, give me a call when you get this message," he said.

He returned to see Stephen sitting at the computer.

"So do any of those places appeal to you? We can always tie in school work with trips we make. Social studies, geography, history, and art are subjects we can explore in any of these places," he said.

"I'll have to think about that," said Stephen. "We've never traveled much, and now we've made two trips in the past couple of weeks."

John's cell phone rang. It was Vanessa.

"Hello," John started to talk, but he didn't say much.

Stephen watched as his smile turned into a more serious expression.

"Yes," said John. "I see."

Stephen raised an eyebrow as he listened to the conversation. It didn't sound good.

"Yes, of course. We'll get there as soon as we can."

John looked at Stephen.

"Lucy's really sick. Vanessa said she took her to the hospital not long after we left. She developed a fever that wouldn't break, and then she started getting other symptoms, headaches, nausea, chills. When she lost consciousness, Vanessa called for an ambulance. The doctors have been running tests, but nothing has come back."

As John spoke, he felt a warmth come into his hands, and they began to tingle.

"I know we just got back, but I told her we'd come. Vanessa doesn't have any other family. She doesn't know what to do," John said.

"I think I'm still packed."

"Me, too. Let's go."

It didn't take long to get back on the road. John wished he hadn't been so obsessed with finding the key that he left without calling Vanessa. He was kicking himself. She needed someone, and he felt like he'd abandoned her.

"You told me that the Gravine hate us because of Elyon," said Stephen. "Besides the nightmares and actually running into them, what do they do? How do they try to destroy us?"

"I've heard of a lot of ways. Gravinder can take bacteria and viruses and mutate them. You've heard of doctors not being able to find the reason for some illnesses; these rare diseases or sickness that people get, and they can't explain them. I believe Gravinder is at the source of them. He converts known viruses and changes it so much that doctors don't even recognize it. It doesn't register in the tests they do on the blood. I'm not a doctor so I don't understand how it works," he replied. "But I do know that we can beat them and their efforts."

While some of the drive back to Vanessa and Lucy was on the interstate, there were a lot of back country roads that the two had to travel on as well. As they were driving on one of these two-lane roads, a deer jumped out in front of their truck. John swerved in an attempt to miss it, but he hit the large animal. The vehicle flipped into a ditch on the side of the road. '

"Stephen. Stephen. Are you okay?" John asked as the truck came to a stop.

It landed right-side up. Fortunately for them, both airbags deployed, and both of them were wearing seatbelts. John could tell Stephen was afraid, but he didn't appear to have any injuries. There were no visible bumps, cuts or bruises.

"Does anything hurt?" John asked.

Stephen shook his head.

"What happened to the deer?" Stephen asked.

"I don't see it. The bumper grazed its back legs. It must have gone to the other side of the road into the woods."

John called emergency services, and he called Vanessa to let her know what had happened.

"We will rent a car, and we will deal with this one when we get back. Don't worry. We are okay. What about Lucy?" he asked.

"The fever won't break. It's still at 104. She's still in a coma, and she doesn't seem to be responding to anything the doctors are doing. They are saying awful things."

John could tell Vanessa was holding back the tears.

"Just hang on. We'll be there as soon as we can."

"What did she say?" Stephen asked.

"No change," John answered.

It wasn't long before the wrecker and police arrived.

"Are you sure you are okay?" the officer asked.

"Yes, we are fine. We were on our way to Tennessee to see a friend whose 9 year-old daughter is in the hospital. We just need to take the truck somewhere and get a rental car as quickly as possible," John explained.

The process of the accident, getting the car to a repair shop, and getting a rental car took several hours out of their day. Stephen was worried about his friend, but he noticed his grandfather seemed to be calm like he knew something but wasn't telling.

"Stephen, what did you learn about the armor? Wasn't there a helmet and a chest protector vest?" John asked.

The question shocked Stephen. He hadn't even thought of that. He wondered what good would it do and how everything was going to work out.

Once they arrived at the hospital, Vanessa met them outside the pediatric intensive care unit. She looked tired, and her eyes were puffy from crying. As soon as she saw John, she hugged him and broke into tears again.

"Vanessa, is there any way I can touch Lucy?" he whispered into her ear.

"Why?"

"Just trust me."

"Stephen will probably have to stay out here," Vanessa said. "There can't be too many people in there at one time, and he's probably too young to go back there."

John turned to look at Stephen.

"It's okay. I won't go anywhere," Stephen said.

"You have to put on a face mask and gown," she said.

Lucy was pale. Her small body had all types of IVs and machines attached to it. John tried to maneuver around the bed to find a place where he could touch her arm. His hands felt like fire as he placed them on her tiny arm. As soon as he touched her, Lucy's eyes flew open, and she gasped for air. It wasn't long before the machines had signaled to the hospital staff the radical changes in her condition. A team of nurses and doctors made their way into the room pushing past John and Vanessa to get to Lucy. Vanessa was confused, but John knew what was happening.

"My baby. What's going on?" said Vanessa as John dragged her out of the room into the waiting area. He led her to a chair and tried to calm her down.

"What happened? What's going on? Why did they all come in there? What did you do to my baby?" Vanessa said on the verge of hysteria.

"Vanessa, calm down. Everything is going to be fine. We will all be leaving this hospital soon."

"What are you talking about?"

"You said you trusted me," he smiled.

She stared at him for a moment with a look of fear. She didn't know what this man had done to her child. Vanessa paced the floor for the next hour and didn't say a word to him.

"She's healed, isn't she?" Stephen leaned over and whispered into his grandfather's ear.

John smiled and nodded.

"I believe she is," John said.

The doctor emerged from the ICU, and Vanessa rushed up to him. He looked puzzled.

"What's the matter?" Vanessa said frantically.

"Nothing ," he said. "We can't find anything wrong with your daughter. The fever's gone. Everything's normal. She's sitting up and asking for French fries like nothing happened. She doesn't have any pain. All of her numbers are normal."

"How is this possible?"

"We don't know. We're going to move her to a regular room, and we want to keep her over the night to monitor her condition. If nothing changes, she can go home in the morning."

"Can I go in and see her?"

"We're getting her ready to transfer her. You can go up to her new room with her," he said.

The doctor turned, and Vanessa followed. It wasn't long before they had Lucy in her own room, and the food was on the way. John and Stephen waited until Vanessa came and got them. She looked stunned but overjoyed.

"She wants to see you, John," said Vanessa.

When John and Stephen got into the room, Lucy was sitting up in bed all smiles. John sat on the edge of the bed, and Lucy hugged him.

"Thank you so much," she said. "When you touched my arm, I felt like I had stuck it into a fire. It was burning, and it brought me back. I don't know how long I was in this place. One of those horrible monsters I was telling you about had its claws around me. It was trying to drag me away. I felt his claws dig into my head and neck. It paralyzed me. I was trying to scream, but it was like no one heard me. Then I saw this huge man. He had dark hair and looked like he worked out at the gym all the time. He was wearing a t-shirt, jeans and boots, but he had this sword. It was made of light or something. They started fighting. I couldn't move. I watched them as they fought. As they fought, I started feeling better, but I still couldn't move. I could hear doctors, and they were saying I might die. When they said that, it seemed like the ugly monster was winning, but when my mom got mad and told them they were wrong; that she wouldn't believe it, the big guy seemed to win."

Lucy looked at John.

"When my mom called you, the monster got mad. He pushed the good guy away, and I saw these other monsters. He sent them after you," she said. "He yelled and told them to kill you. They kept fighting until you came and touched my arm. Then another one showed up. He had red hair and freckles just like me. He and the other guy pushed their swords through the monster. He screamed and left," Lucy said.

Lucy looked at her mother.

"I'm hungry," she said.

"They are going to bring you food, honey," said Vanessa.

All of this talk of monsters made Vanessa's head spin. One minute her daughter was dying and the next, she was sitting up asking for food.

"John, could we go outside for a minute?" Vanessa asked.

They walked out of the hospital room and into an empty waiting area.

"What is she talking about?" Vanessa asked. "What did you do to her?"

"I tried to tell you a little about the Gravine. I can't really talk about that here. I do want to tell you more," he said. "The doctor said she could leave tomorrow. We will have plenty of time to talk. She is going to be just fine."

"How can you be sure?"

"I'm going to teach you what I know. This was just to keep you from accomplishing what is supposed to be accomplished."

"I don't know if I want to do this," said Vanessa.

"It's okay. You need some rest. When was the last time you slept?"

"Sleep? I don't even know what that is."

"Let's get you something to eat, and then you can get some rest."

"You're right. The past two months have almost been more than I could bear, and I still have to clean my mother's house to get it ready to sell. Lucy has missed so much school," Vanessa said.

"Everything will be okay," he said and tried to smile.

She took a deep breath and nodded.

"Thank you for everything. I can't believe how kind you've been to us," said Vanessa.

"Stephen and I will stay overnight; just call me if you need anything," he said. "We have a hotel room not far from here."

11

Stephen had been quiet for most of the hospital visit, but he was just keeping a lot inside so he could talk with his grandfather.

"You knew all along that Lucy was going to be fine, didn't you?" Stephen asked as soon as they got into the car.

"Yes. I did. I had a dream last night about your key and the healing gift that flows through me."

"When did you first realize you had this gift, and why haven't you been using it?"

That remark stung John.

"I was about your age. We were playing baseball after school one day. One of the boys hit a line drive right back at the pitcher whose name was Billy. It hit Billy in the face and flattened him on his back. It wasn't an organized game; it was just a bunch of us playing so there weren't any adults around. A couple of the boys ran to get help. Everyone else just stood there not really knowing what to do. I went over to Billy. He wasn't moving. The ball hit him right above the eye. There was a cut and a lump over his eye. I felt my hands heat up like I was holding them close to a fire. The palms were burning. It was like slow-motion. I reached down and touched him on the head. The cut and lump immediately disappeared. He opened his eyes and sat up. No one really saw what I did, but I knew and Billy knew," he said. "As far as your second question, there have been a lot of things I've known to do and have not done. I've been coming to terms with that over the past few weeks. I have a second chance, and I'm taking it."

"You know I saw the Gravine at our house before. Why didn't I see them at Lucy's grandma's house? I mean, they must have been there because she got sick right after we left? She described them to us."

"Remember what I said about them waiting until you weren't paying attention? That's what they do. They conceal themselves. Out of sight; out of mind. That's something they like to do. You have to constantly be on guard - not looking for them all the time or thinking they've caused every problem because that's not true. But be alert. Be aware," said John.

"It sounds like they may have caused our accident. Lucy said they wanted to kill us."

"They must have scared the deer causing it to rush out in front of us when it did. It delayed us for a while, but it's all going to work out."

Stephen was quiet for a few minutes.

"Do you like Vanessa?" Stephen asked.

John was surprised. He wondered if he had been that obvious.

"I don't know how to answer that question. She needs us right now. She's going through a rough time, and I don't really know her that well," John answered. "Why do you ask?"

"I just think that there might be more than one reason that we've met her and Lucy."

"And what do you mean by that?"

"Grown-ups want to be in love. Don't you?"

"I suppose. My job is taking care of you. And as far as Vanessa, I don't know the answer to that question," John said. "Let's just wait and see what happens. We can't rush into anything."

"I know. She's really nice when she's not crying. I'd like to be around her when she's not crying. She does smile when she looks at you, and you are looking back at her."

"It's been tough for her and Lucy lately. I'd like to see more smiles from her too."

"I bet she is funny," Stephen said.

"Why do you say that?"

"Because Lucy is very funny. Her mom must be funny, too."

"I hope we get to find out soon."

"Me too, Papa," Stephen said.

The next morning, John waited for Vanessa's phone call. John and Stephen were having breakfast around 9 when the phone rang.

"Hi," said an excited voice over the phone. "Lucy gets to leave this morning!"

"Yes. We were expecting to hear that," said John.

"You have been so kind to us; we want to do something for you today. We definitely want to take you to lunch or dinner."

"That sounds good. Stephen and I are going to do some sightseeing in Gatlinburg today. Would you like to go with us?"

"I think we'd like that very much," she said. "As soon as we get our paper work filled out, I'll give you a call."

A few hours later, the quartet arrived in Gatlinburg.

"You know I've lived here all my life, but I've never done all the touristy things," said Vanessa.

It was an unseasonably warm winter day. They visited the museums and the tourist shops.

"Since you are here, we have to visit the Gatlinburg Space Needle," said Vanessa. "It's not Seattle, but it's fun."

"Sounds good to me," said Stephen.

They took the glass elevators 400 feet to the observation deck, where they could see a panoramic view of the area. Even though it was winter, the view of the Smoky Mountains was breathtaking.

"You should visit here during the fall. The colors are incredible," said Vanessa. "It's like God took a palette of golds, reds, and yellows and painted the trees in these vivid hues. There is not a more beautiful place. Spring is incredible too. You just happened to come in between."

"That's okay," said John. "This view now is beautiful. What do you think Stephen?"

"You can see everything here. This is great," Stephen said.

"Hey, for supper, let's go somewhere away from the hustle and bustle of tourist life. I know a great restaurant where we can have some good, down-home cooking," she said.

"That's just fine with me," said John.

"I'm hungry," said Stephen.

John smiled at Stephen.

"You're always hungry," said John. "I guess that's part of being a growing almost teenager. The next few years ought to bring an interesting grocery bill."

"I like country cooking," he said.

"So do I," said Vanessa. "They have amazing fried chicken and chicken and dumplings. The summer time is best because they have a vegetable garden, or they buy produce from local farmers. Fresh corn on the cob, sliced red tomatoes, black-eyed peas, and peach cobbler for dessert. Now, I'm getting hungry."

"Yea. You need to stop," said Stephen. "My mouth is watering."

"I'm getting hungry," said Lucy.

"Let's go," Vanessa said.

The restaurant was just like she said. It was rustic and off the beaten trail. The owner of the restaurant was a lady named Betty. Although she was in her 70s, there was an ageless quality about her. Her sunny personality was what people immediately noticed about her. She was once the cook too, but she left the cooking to her daughter, Bobbie, and Bobbie's husband, Ray. Betty liked to be out in the front of the restaurant, meeting customers as they came in.

"Vanessa, sweetie, it's so good to see you," Betty hugged Vanessa when she arrived. "I was sorry to hear about your mama. She was a good woman."

"Thank you, Betty. I think I remember seeing you at the funeral, but it was such a blur," she said.

"I know, and Lucy, what a big girl you are now," said Betty.

"Betty, these are our friends, John and Stephen. I've been telling them all about your country cooking, and they are looking forward to trying it," said Vanessa.

"Well, you just sit right down, and I'll get you started with some of my famous sweet tea and homemade biscuits," said Betty.

"John, I needed to talk to you about what happened with Lucy, but this won't be the place. I didn't even think about that when I told you about coming here. Betty will probably join us at some point during the meal," Vanessa said and laughed. "She and my mother knew each other very well."

"I understand," he said.

Betty brought out a big basket of biscuits with butter and a pitcher of sweet tea, and just as Vanessa said, Betty sat down with them.

"How have you been doing, sweetie?" Betty asked.

"It's been hard the past few weeks," said Vanessa.

"Yes, I understand. It's hard to lose your mama."

"Betty, did you know my mother was an artist?"

Betty's face lit up.

"Oh yes, she was wonderful, but that father of yours. I don't want to speak ill of the dead, but he was a mean one. He was one way to the world, but to the people close to him, especially your mama – God rest her soul – he was awful. I don't know why she stayed with him. She was such a gifted woman, but he didn't want the world to see what a gift she was. And the pictures she painted. Oh my. It was like they were from another world. Well, I guess they were. The stories she used to tell me. They were wonderful too – amazing really."

"What stories did she tell you?"

"You father didn't like them either. He used to call her a fool, and he didn't want her telling anyone because he thought they'd think she was a crazy woman," said Betty. "She used to tell me stories about the Jeweled City."

Vanessa almost choked on a biscuit.

"Why didn't she ever tell me any of these things? Lucy has been there. Lucy and Mama went there together right before she died," Vanessa said.

Betty smiled.

"The Jeweled City is a real place. It's beautiful," Betty said softly as her voice trailed off. It was as if she were visiting there in her mind as she spoke. "She didn't tell you because of your father, but Elyon always told her that after she died, he'd make sure your place in his kingdom would be secure."

Vanessa's mouth dropped, and she simply stared at Betty.

"I'll be right back," Betty said, and she headed off toward the kitchen.

"I guess we can talk about what you wanted to talk about?" John said and chuckled.

"I think I'm the only person in the world who hasn't heard of Elyon," said Vanessa.

"No, Mama, you aren't, but that's okay," said Lucy.

"The more I find out, the more this bothers me," said Vanessa. "I feel like my entire life has been a lie."

"Vanessa, Stephen and I know that we are supposed to reach Elyon's people who are scattered. Some of them have been born into that family, and they don't even know it. Our job is to wake them up to who they are, and the inheritance they have," said John. "You obviously are one of them. And then, you and Lucy will be sent to wake up others."

"I'm so confused," she said.

"Don't let it overwhelm you," he said. "It can only get you down if you let it."

Betty seemed to have been gone for a long time. She finally reappeared holding a box in her hands.

"Sweetie, your mama asked me to hold on to this until she was gone. There are a lot of things that you will learn in here. She didn't want to keep things from you, and she tried over the years to explain things to you. You didn't understand. You thought she was confused. You even thought she was crazy at times. She did tell Lucy things. She loved Lucy so," said Betty.

"Betty, Stephen and John know of Elyon, too. They've both been to the Jeweled City," said Vanessa.

"Oh, I know. I could tell the minute they walked in the door," Betty said and smiled. "There's just something special about the two of them. He's a good man, Vanessa, a very good man."

Betty turned and pointed at John.

"He's got a good heart. It's been wounded, but it's been healing too. He will take good care of you and Lucy. Don't let him get away. Now, I'm back to the kitchen. Your food should just about be finished."

Vanessa felt her cheeks turning red.

"I'm sorry about that," Vanessa said obviously flustered by Betty's words.

"There's nothing to be sorry about, Vanessa," said John.

"How long are you planning on staying here? You've got to see about your truck, and I'm sure that you have things you have to do," she said.

"Are you trying to get rid of us now?" he asked, half-joking.

"No, no. Not at all. I know you can't stay here forever," she said.

"I can stay as long as you need me too," he said.

"Well, I think Miss Betty is right. I like them, and I think we should keep them. I would like to have a daddy, and I've always wanted a brother," said Lucy.

"Lucy," Vanessa said. "That's enough."

Now, it was John's turn to blush.

"Miss Betty has always 'known things' that's what Nana said. Nana told me that Miss Betty would say things about the future, and they'd happen. She also can tell a lot about a person just by being around them. Nana said she was never wrong," said Lucy.

Vanessa turned to John.

"Lucy spent all of her summers here from the time she was old enough to talk," said Vanessa. "She knows the people in this town better than I did or do now. I knew Betty, but not as well as Lucy apparently does."

Betty brought out a heaping portion of fried chicken for all of them to share. There were other side dishes such as corn on the cob, black-eyed peas, collard greens and mashed potatoes.

"Miss Betty, are you going to join us?" John asked.

"I'd be delighted," she said. "You four would make a fine-looking family.""So, Miss Betty. What else can you tell us?" John inquired.

"John, I could tell you a lot of things, but the biggest thing I can tell you is that your past is behind you. You aren't an extremely young man, but you still have a lot of living to do. Your job isn't just to raise Stephen to fulfill his mission. You still have a destiny you must achieve. Your latter years will be so much better than your youth. You have a lot to look forward to," she said.

John felt tears well up in his eyes.

"Don't look back any more," she said. "Look straight ahead of you. And as for you, Stephen, you stay close to your grandfather's side for the next few years. He will guide you, and he won't steer you in the wrong direction. In the next few months, you will find yourself wanting to challenge him and wanting to do your own thing. Follow him until you fully come of age, and even then, your grandfather will be there to give you wisdom."

"How did you know he was my grandfather? Most people think he's my dad," said Stephen.

"I told you, Stephen; she knows things," Lucy elbowed Stephen and whispered to him. "Just because I'm 9 years-old people don't listen to me."

"Little Lucy, you are such a light. The experience you came out of with the Gravine that put you in the hospital will only make you stronger," said Betty.

Lucy smiled.

"See, what did I tell you? She knows stuff without us even saying," said Lucy, who had a big smile on her face.

"Lucy, that's your gift too. You will know things about people, and you will know things before they happen," said Betty. "At this table are many gifts. There's healing and wisdom in John. There's knowing and seeing in Lucy. There's leadership and vision in Stephen.

Stephen can also see into Elyon's realm with a lot of sharpness, and he's a warrior."

She looked straight into Stephen's eyes.

"You just have to develop that gift," she said.

Then she looked at Vanessa, who was getting more and more uncomfortable by the minute.

"And Vanessa, there's much compassion and sensitivity in you. And whether you realize it or not, you can see into the future too. You try to figure things out with your head too much, and you can't do that all the time. The four of you working together would be a great team, and you already know that in your heart," she said. "Well, I see that it's time for dessert."

She got up and left the table.

Soon, she came back with several bowls of piping hot peach cobbler covered in vanilla bean ice cream.

The kids dug into the dessert with gusto. Vanessa just wanted to get out of the restaurant. She felt as though her feelings had been placed on her sleeve, and it made her uncomfortable. She didn't think she was over Charlie yet; maybe she was. She was confused because she did have some feelings stirring for John. He wasn't like anyone she'd ever met before.

Vanessa couldn't look at John.

"Vanessa, Stephen and I will leave in the morning if you want us to," said John. "Do you want to go ahead and go to the car? I'll get the bill."

Vanessa and Lucy headed to the car without saying anything.

As he paid the check, Betty spoke to him.

"You know that I'm right. Sometimes, I'm a little outspoken, but I don't hold back on my words. Life is too short to waste time and pitter-patter around the obvious. I'm an old woman, and I can't wait around. I have to say what I know. You're a good man, John, and you deserve that second chance at love. You would be good for her, and she has feelings for you even though she doesn't want to admit it yet. She will come around. Mark my words," said Betty.

John smiled.

"Deep in my heart, I believe you are right, but Vanessa will have to come to that decision on her own," he said. "I hope she won't take too long to discover what's in her heart."

Betty gave him a hug.

"Trust your instincts with Stephen. You will do what's right. You didn't fail your son even though you think you did. Stephen may not be your son, but he's got more of you in him than your son did," she said.

John got a little teary.

"It's going to be just fine, John," Betty said.

"Thank you," he said.

It was a quiet drive back to Vanessa's homestead.

"John, could I talk with you?" she asked.

"Of course," he answered.

"Lucy, it's time for you to go to bed," she said. "Stephen, you can watch television. We don't have any video games or a computer or anything."

"It's okay. I have my phone."

John nodded.

"Would you like a cup of coffee?" she asked John.

"No, thanks. It's getting a little late for that, and I don't think I could add anything else to my stomach after that incredible meal. I haven't had food like that in a very long time," he said and followed her into the kitchen.

She made a cup of coffee for herself and sat down.

"Listen, about the things that Betty said," she started.

"You don't have to say anything," John answered. "You have to search your heart."

"I've never considered a relationship since Charlie died," she said.

"Vanessa, you don't have to explain anything," he said. "Don't feel like you have to explain. This is all sudden, and I'm not the type of person to rush into anything."

"I know. It's the craziest thing. We barely know each other, but

I feel like I've known you all of my life. I have never felt this way about anyone else. I thought it was love at first sight with Charlie, but this is so different. There was this wild attraction at first. I guess you couldn't really call that love at first sight. Over the next few years, it changed. It was more than chemistry. There was a strong, unbreakable bond. I felt he was part of my heart and soul. Don't take this the wrong way, but the first time I saw you it wasn't with the thought of how handsome you were. It was with the thought of how wonderful a husband you would be. Insane, yes, I know. Not a thought you have about everyone. With you, it was like you've always been a part of me. You immediately went into that heart and soul place. I felt a connection on such a deeper level than a physical chemistry with you. I can't believe I'm saying any of this. It was the way I felt about Charlie after we'd been married. That feeling of home. He was home for me. And now, you feel like home to me. And I feel like I'm betraying him and me and everyone. For Betty to say all of those things, it was hard to hear because I wanted to say them so badly. I couldn't believe she was pulling my thoughts out of my head, and I don't even know how you feel. You must think I'm crazy and that Betty is crazy. Maybe, it's stress and emotional overload."

"I understood what Betty said," he said. "I shut myself down after my wife left me. Emotionally, I had steel walls and concertina wire around my heart. I never allowed anyone in in more than 30 years. I had well-meaning friends who tried to find dates for me, but in my heart, no one ever compared to Meredith even though she was totally wrong for me. Then, I met you. A couple of months ago, I still had pain when I thought of her. There was still regret and anger. When all of this happened with Stephen, the pain began to disappear. Just a few days ago, I found the letter she wrote when she left. I realized all my tears had been cried."

"So what do we do?" she asked.

"I'm not sure, but I am old-fashioned. We have plenty of time to figure this all out. No one needs to make any decisions about anything right now. I would like to get to know you better," he said.

John smiled.

"Stephen and I will stay another day, but then we will go home. I will give you time to figure out what it is you want. You have to sort things out. You have the grief of your mother and the discoveries about her life. You have to figure out Lucy's future because I must go back to my home. If you feel the words of Betty were true, then you know how to reach me. I will be there to talk to you. We can get to know each other through phone calls and emails. I can come back here and visit. But I don't want to do anything that will cloud your emotions right now. You have had a lot going on over the past few months," he said.

"Betty is right about one thing," she said. "You are a very good man. I can honestly say I've never met anyone like you. Most people are only out for themselves. I've met a lot of selfish men in my time."

"Thank you."

He leaned over and kissed her forehead.

"Go get some sleep, and don't call me until after noon. You are exhausted physically and mentally."

"You're right. I can think about all that tomorrow."

Stephen and John got in the car to head back to the hotel.

"So if you marry Vanessa, she'd be my grandmother, and Lucy would be my aunt?" asked Stephen. "That's weird since she's younger than I am."

"No one is getting married right now, but yes, Lucy would be your aunt if something happened."

"What did you think about what Betty had to say to us?" Stephen asked.

"I wish I had recorded it, but I did write down a lot of the things she told us. She was right about some things she said. I'm interested to see how it all turns out."

"Did you ask Vanessa to marry you?" asked Stephen.

"No. It's a little more complicated than that."

"Well, she likes you, and you like her. That doesn't sound complicated to me. Adults just make things harder than they should be."

John shook his head and laughed.

12

John was up early the next morning. He called to check on his truck, and he was curious about the emails he'd been getting seemingly out of nowhere. He had brought his laptop, and there were more emails. They all asked the same questions. They were asking him to come and tell them about fighting the Gravine.

Stephen woke up and saw John at the computer.

"What time is it?" he asked.

"It's 7:15. The garage opened at 6:30. The truck should be repaired by the end of the week."

"What are you doing on the computer?" Stephen asked.

"I was just going through these emails. I have 10 new emails asking us to come and tell them about the Gravine. How are these people getting my email address? I don't understand all of this, but I actually feel like I may have to respond to a few of these. I don't know everything there is to know, but I guess there is something I have to offer."

"Well, you said that not one person could do this. It was going take a lot of people."

"Yes, this is true," John said. "Ever since you went through the book into the other world, nothing makes sense any more so I guess people I don't know sending me emails fits the pattern."

"I didn't know what saying 'yes' to him would mean for both of us."

"I had said 'yes' a long, long time ago, but I had forgotten about it."

"So, do you have any ideas about where we are supposed to go?"

"I'm not sure yet. The emails all seem to say about the same thing. They all have had similar encounters, but they don't know what it all means," John said. "What about you? Have you had any dreams or other thoughts lately that might give us a clue?"

"Actually, I have," said Stephen. "Well, I was reading in the book for a little while before we left to come here to see Lucy in the hospital. All of a sudden, I saw this picture in my head of mountains and people with black hair. They were wearing really bright colors, and they had these animals with these long necks, but they weren't as long as giraffes. They were furry too. They looked a little like camels."

"Stephen, that sounds like Peru. Those animals were probably alpaca or llamas or both."

"Cool. We're going to Peru."

"First things first. We will have to get passports to travel into another country. We aren't going to rush into anything, but I think we will know exactly where we are supposed to go and when we are supposed to be there," John said. "I think we will be busy when we get back home."

"When are we going home?"

"Probably today," said John. "We will get breakfast and check out of the hotel. I will check on Vanessa and Lucy, and then I think we need to go home."

"So, do you have any emails from Peru?"

"No, I don't. How is your Spanish?"

"I know how to count to 10," Stephen said.

"Well, if we are supposed to go there, then I guess language won't be a problem. We'll figure it out."

"The Book of Ancient Wisdom was written in another language, but we don't have any problems reading it."

"Good point. We've got a job to do so we will work out the details. I'm sure we could find an interpreter if necessary."

While John and Stephen got breakfast, Vanessa got up from a long night of tossing and turning. She was exhausted, but sleep seemed to be far away. She had so many things on her mind.

She went into the hidden room in her mother's house and sat there looking at the paintings. She found several letters in the box Betty had given to her. They were from her mother and written to Vanessa. They explained a lot, but Vanessa still had questions. Unlike Lucy and her mother, Vanessa had never met Elyon. She felt like the outcast in all of it. Everyone else had been to this Jeweled City. She gazed at the paintings. They were so real. The colors were so vivid. As she was sitting there in her pajama pants and sweatshirt, Lucy came into the room and sat on the floor next to her. She put her head on her mother's arm.

"Why aren't you resting?" Vanessa asked Lucy.

"Oh, Mama. The doctors said I was fine yesterday. There's nothing wrong with me."

"Yes, I guess you are right."

"Are we going to see John and Stephen today?"

"I don't know. All of this is moving so quickly. I never thought about dating anyone or getting married again. I need for this to go a little slower, and John said that was okay."

"Miss Betty is always right when she starts talking like that. You should listen to her. It shouldn't be that hard."

"Lucy, I do love you," Vanessa said and laughed.

"Mom, you know you aren't getting any younger."

"Lucy, thanks a lot. It's great to know I'm so decrepit," Vanessa said.

"Mama, I'm only 9. Everyone older than 12 is old to me. Besides, you like Mr. John. I know you do."

"I am not having this discussion with you. It's okay to like someone and not run off and marry them when you've only known them a short period of time."

"Whatever, Mom. When are they leaving?"

"Today, but I don't know when."

"Please call him. I like Stephen. He doesn't think I'm crazy, and he believes me when I tell him things. Other kids don't," Lucy pleaded.

"What time is it? I was given strict orders to sleep until after noon."

"It's about 10:15."

"Then, we'll wait."

The doorbell rang. Vanessa looked at Lucy.

"You didn't invite anyone over, did you?" Vanessa asked.

"Nope, not me."

At the door was a delivery from a local flower shop. It was a large flower arrangement with a mix of red roses, stargazer lilies and white carnations.

"Those are pretty. Who are they from?" Lucy asked as she jumped up and down.

Vanessa took the arrangement to the living room and placed them on the coffee table. She took the card and sat down.

I look forward to what the future might hold - John, read the card.

"These are from John," said Vanessa.

"See, I told you he liked you."

"Yes, and I like him as well."

Vanessa's cell phone rang. It was John.

"Hello. The flowers just arrived. They are amazing. Thank you so much," she said.

"Somehow, I didn't think you'd take my advice to sleep until the afternoon," he said.

"I'm sorry. There's just too much going on."

"I'm glad you like the flowers."

"Thank you. All of them are my favorites," she said.

"Would you like to have lunch before we leave? We won't go to Betty's, I promise."

Vanessa laughed.

"That's a good idea. We can be ready in about an hour," she said.

"It sounds good. I'd really like a steak."

"I know just the place," she said.

She hung up the phone and quickly headed back upstairs to find something to wear. Lucy watched her mother. She was happy, and Lucy liked that. She'd seen her mother cry a lot over the past few weeks. It was hard on her.

"You should wear something green. It makes you look pretty," Lucy said.

"Green? You think so?" said Vanessa, searching for something pretty and green. "All of my really nice things are at home. Do you think we have time to shop?"

Lucy shook her head.

"I've been shopping with you. You take a long time to decide things," Lucy said.

"You're right. Well, how about this green sweater and black pants?"

"That's pretty."

"Okay. I'm going to take a shower. You get dressed," Vanessa said.

Vanessa was still putting on make-up when Lucy ran into the room.

"They're here. They're here," she said. "Come on, Mama. Let's go."

"Go to the door, and I will be there shortly."

Lucy ran downstairs and opened the door, hugging both John and Stephen.

"Mama is making herself pretty," said Lucy.

Vanessa walked down the stairs about the same time Lucy finished that sentence.

"And Lucy, you would be right," said John. "She looks very pretty."

"Ready for some steak?" Vanessa asked. "I know a great place. It's not a chain, and Betty doesn't work there."

"Let's go," said John.

The restaurant looked like an old cabin, but it had some very unusual décor. Stephen noticed something as soon as they came in.

"Papa," he said. "Look at the walls."

John looked around. There were travel posters on the wall, and they looked really old. One of the posters showed Peru with mountains and alpaca. He looked at Stephen.

"I'll check it out when we get home," he said. "I think we are right on track."

"What is it?" asked Vanessa, as they were seated.

"You know how we traveled and met you. Well, Stephen and I feel that we may be going some other places as well as we continue on our quest," said John. "Peru keeps coming up."

"Really? So far away," Vanessa said.

"We don't know how long or when we will go," he answered.

"Will that keep you from coming back here?"

"I'm sure you and I will see each other again,"

Vanessa smiled.

"The flowers are gorgeous. Thank you so much. I haven't had flowers delivered to my doorstep in years," she said.

"You're very welcome. Obviously, this isn't like any relationship you've ever had," he said and laughed. He looked at the two children with them at the table.

"No, it's not, but I think it's something I could get used to quickly," she said and smiled.

John nodded.

"Me, too."

After lunch, John and Stephen spent the next several hours talking about their task and how the book was giving them insight into what they needed to do. The book also contained information on Elyon's realm and how to get ready for what was going to take place.

"I don't have all the answers. Some things seem hard to understand, but that's when you step out on the little you know. The rest works out somehow," said John. "What we have to do is gather, in a metaphorical sense, Elyon's people together. When he returns, he will gather them physically."

"There's so much to remember," she said.

"The book is vital. It is the doorway from his realm to ours. You can find answers there If you need anything, I'm a phone call away."

"Thank you."

The drive back home was relatively quiet. Stephen looked up information on Peru on his phone.

"These are such big places. Where exactly in Peru are we supposed to go?" Stephen asked.

"I will check my email when we get home. We probably have a request from there."

"How long do you think it will be before you get married? I like them, but things will change. It won't be just you and me anymore."

"Stephen, no one is getting married. You'll be the first one I tell after I ask someone. Okay? And if that happens, I will always make time for you. You are more important to me than you can ever know. Nothing will change that, and you have to remember that."

"I know. I've never had a mom that I can remember. You're the only dad I've known. I can't imagine what it will be like to have a woman living with us, and to have a mom or grandma or whatever she will be."

"It will take some getting used to, but it will be a good thing if it happens. Just because Betty said we're getting married doesn't mean it's going to happen tomorrow or even happen at all," he said.

It was late when they arrived home, but John went directly into the library.

Lemachor was lurking in the background. He was becoming increasingly agitated by all of the movement with John. The change from John's laidback, do-nothing-important life to becoming a man of action was disturbing. The tricks of the past weren't working as well. Bringing up the memories of the pain of rejection that had paralyzed John for years weren't working. Putting distractions in front of him weren't working, but Lemachor knew John well enough to know his Achilles' heel.

It had been a long few days for Stephen, and he had fallen asleep a few times in the car. He wasn't really sleepy when he got home, but he didn't follow his grandfather into the library. As he lay in bed, he thought about what it might be like to go to Peru. He'd read a book about Peru. It was still on his shelf, but he wanted to know more. That night, he dreamed of Peru. He and John were in a small village. He could see mountains all around them, and it was very cold – colder than anything he'd ever experienced. He and John had backpacks and seemed to be hiking through the region when a man rushed up to them.

Stephen woke up. He looked at the clock. It was about 2 a.m. He peeked into the hallway to see if his grandfather was still awake. He was not really surprised to see the lights were still on in the library so he walked in to find his grandfather reading the book with pen and paper next to him.

"Papa," he said.

John looked up.

"What are you doing up? What time is it?" John asked and looked at the clock.

"I had this dream I need to tell you about," he said. "It was very short, but I think it is important."

"Okay, go ahead," said John.

John listened and wrote down a couple of things on a pad of paper.

"Winter in Peru is our summer," said John when he finished. "There are no emails from Peru or from South America at all. Summer is still a few months away, but that doesn't really mean anything at this point. I'll keep checking."

13

Winter turned into spring.

John and Vanessa spent long hours on the phone each day. Stephen knew what Miss Betty had said was going to happen. It was just a matter of when. Stephen could tell in the way his grandfather's voice changed when he talked about Vanessa. Stephen and Lucy talked about it a lot. They liked the idea of being related. She thought the idea of being his aunt was funny.

When they weren't visiting Vanessa and Lucy, they spent a lot of time learning about the book. Watching the words come up out of the pages and form sentences above him wowed Stephen every time, and he also spent time learning how to use the armor.

The Gravine had been quiet, but Stephen still knew they were there. He saw them lurking in the hallway near the library. They didn't know he saw them. They thought they were able to hide in time. They weren't as quick as they thought. Stephen thought about what John had told him - how they were always looking for an opportunity. Sometimes, they had to wait until the right moment to strike. Stephen wondered what they were planning.

Stephen also spent a lot of time reading the journals his ancestors wrote. They had many adventures. They would dream about going to a place they'd never been, and even though they didn't know anything about the place, they'd just go. They'd meet interesting people along the way. Sometimes, it would be dangerous because there were renegades on the road who wanted to rob them, but the Enkeli would hide Stephen's ancestors. At other times, strange things would happen. Once they went into the Texas territory as they called it in the journal. They were being chased by bandits, and a dust storm came out of nowhere. Stephen's great-great-great-grandfather wrote that he saw the Enkeli running around the bandits in circles stirring up the dust.

Emails continued to flood in from all parts of the country and the globe. Stephen and John made a couple of trips within driving distance. They traveled to meet a cattle rancher in Texas and a barbecue restaurant owner in Mississippi. They wanted to test things out before they went to Peru and other countries.

Stephen wasn't sure how his grandfather went without sleep, and as the clock hit 2 a.m. again, he decided to see what John was up to. He looked down the hallway, and the library door was open.

"Why are you up so late?" Stephen asked.

"I've just been thinking about things," John answered. "And I went on a search for something special among the heirlooms we have in a safe in the house."

John pulled out a two-carat oval ruby ring with diamonds encircling it.

"It originally belonged to my great-grandmother, your great-great-grandmother, but it has been passed down through the family line. It was supposed to go to the woman I married. My parents didn't approve of your grandmother so I didn't get to give it to her. I found it after they died. Do you think Vanessa would like it?" John asked.

"Wow. That's some ring. It's really pretty," he said.

"Usually, women want diamonds as engagement rings, but Vanessa has been married before. She probably had a diamond," John said. "I didn't think I'd ever give it to anyone except maybe to you for you to give to someone."

"I think she would like that it belonged to someone in our family. She seems to be that kind of person. You know, someone who likes things with a story attached to them. And it's different."

John stared at the ring.

"When are you going to ask her? I wonder if she'll say 'yes,'" said Stephen.

"I hope she does. I'm planning something special not too long from now. We've gotten to know each other pretty well over the past few months. It might be time to ask her."

"Well, it's like Lucy says. You aren't getting any younger."

"Thanks for reminding me," John said. "Well, it's late. Come on. You need your rest."

Vanessa also spent a lot of time thinking about Betty's prophecy. She didn't want to rush anything, but marrying John seemed like the right thing to do. She could see herself growing old with him, and she believed he'd be a good father to Lucy. She'd been taking her time settling her mother's affairs. She wasn't in any hurry. There were 50 years of memories to clean out, and it seemed almost everything brought up memories. Vanessa liked that she had John to help her through her grief even if he lived a few hours away. In a way, she was glad he didn't live close by. She needed to process the death of her mother and the revelation of Elyon. She also had to think about what Betty had said to her about a relationship with John. The more she thought about it, the more she agreed.

As she was packing some items in a box to give away the following afternoon, she heard a knock on the door. She discovered a man in a business suit there.

"Hello, ma'am. I'm James D. Braswell. I represent a group of investors who have heard about your mother's passing and are interested in purchasing her home and the surrounding acreage for a resort."

Vanessa was puzzled.

"Would you like to come in?" she asked.

"No, thank you, that won't be necessary. I won't stay long," he said. "I have a formal proposal, which I would like to leave with you for the purchase of the house and the property. Enclosed you will find my card and phone number. My investors understand you are going through a difficult time right now, and they do not require an immediate answer. If you find the offer acceptable, then they are prepared to give you payment immediately. And if there are items in the house you simply want to dispose of, we can also hand that for you. Please feel free to call at any time."

Mr. Braswell handed her a manila envelope.

"Have a good day," he said.

"Thank you. You too."

He headed toward his car. Vanessa hadn't even thought about putting the house on the market. It wasn't dilapidated, but it needed some fixing up. She thought she'd have to do some of that before considering the sale. She went back inside and opened the manila envelope. She thumbed through the paperwork and almost dropped it on the floor when she saw the amount of money they were offering her.

The home was out off the beaten path and sat on about 10 acres of land. It had an amazing view, and she could see now how it could be considered a great place for vacationers. Still stunned, she picked up her cell phone and called John.

"Hi," she said. "You won't believe what just happened. Someone came out of the blue and asked to buy my parents' home."

"That's great. Did you want to sell it?" he asked.

"I think so. I still have a home back in Nashville that I need to do something with," she said. "You should see how much money they are offering for this place."

"Do you have a lawyer who can review it for you?"

"Yes, there is a lawyer who was friends of my parents for many years. He's helped me with my mother's and father's wills."

"It sounds like everything is falling in line. If you need me to help you finish up there, let me know. I can make another trip soon," he said.

"Well, I thought I'd give you a little bit of time. I know you had some things to take care of back home, and there's Stephen to think about too."

"Stephen is fine. He is enrolled in classes online so his school goes wherever he and his laptop go," he said. "How's Lucy?"

"She's really enjoying the online school thing too. I'm glad you suggested it."

"Great. Speaking of that, I'm going to check on Stephen. He had a test this morning."

John headed to the library to check on Stephen.

"So what are you learning today?" John asked.

"You won't believe it. I'm moving into a section on geography and topography studying the various mountain chains in North and South America. Look at the photos of the Andes Mountains," Stephen said and pointed to the screen.

"Let me check my email. We haven't heard anything from Peru yet."

Stephen continued to read about geography, but his mind went back to the armor they'd received. John hadn't talked about it much, and the Gravine were still quiet. Stephen hadn't had a chance to test it out. He thought about the battles he'd had with the Gravine so far and wondered where they were hiding. School was boring, he thought. Fighting ugly-looking creatures was much more interesting. He looked around the room. He didn't see anything out of his realm. Everything looked still and quiet.

Was this what Papa talked about? They stay quiet planning their next round of attacks? he thought.

Lemachor was indeed gathering his troops and biding his time. He didn't feel the need to rush especially since Gravinder wasn't breathing down his neck. Stephen and John hadn't made too many waves for them yet. Maybe Vanessa had been the distraction John needed after all.

"I thought they'd forgotten about Peru," Lemachor said to the Gravine gathered round him. "Peru is important. It will change the course of things. If they spark the people in Peru, they will set off a chain reaction that cannot be stopped. I've heard from our cohorts in Peru that they've kept a band of Elyon's people under severe circumstances for many years. There are other groups of people across the world, who are Elyon's people, and we've been able to keep them under for generations. Stephen's little escapade into Africa started a few fires, but we have them contained for now. All these other people need is a spark to awaken them. There has been a growing dissatisfaction in them. They want their lives to change. We have to stop this chain reaction from happening. John's main weakness is fear - fear of being abandoned and of losing everything important to him. Now, we can see that in addition to Stephen, there are others who are becoming important to him. Bandion and his group struck against Lucy, but he failed on purpose. He gave up quickly in order to give John a false sense of confidence in his abilities. We will strike again, and when we do, we won't give up so easily. We will be joining forces with others to make sure we stop Stephen and his grandfather."

14

John and Stephen were going to be in town visiting Vanessa and Lucy again. Even though she'd gotten used to it, there was something about this visit that caused butterflies in the pit of Vanessa's stomach. Vanessa was looking forward to this visit even more than usual, and she wasn't sure why. She couldn't explain it. Vanessa felt giddy like a teenager again. She looked out the window every few minutes in hopes of seeing his truck in the driveway.

"Mom, they'll be here. Stop worrying," said Lucy.

She didn't realize that Lucy had noticed her pacing and constant trips to the window. It wasn't long before a Mercedes pulled up in the driveway. She wasn't sure who that could possibly be, but as she looked out the window, she noticed John and Stephen get out of the car, and John helping Betty out of the vehicle as well. Vanessa was shocked to see John wearing a tuxedo and holding what looked to be a garment bag. Stephen was carrying a bouquet of red roses.

"What is all of this?" Vanessa asked as she opened the door.

"Miss Betty has agreed to take the night off from the restaurant to stay here with Stephen and Lucy," he said.

She smiled.

He held out the garment bag.

"And this is for you. Betty helped me pick your size. We're going on a date," he said with a big smile.

Lucy excitedly followed her mother upstairs. Vanessa took the garment bag upstairs and tried on the dress. It was a knee-length black dress with a sweetheart neckline and sheer sleeves. She tried it on, and it fit perfectly. Inside the bag were a pair of black pumps and a box with a pair of crystal earrings.

"You look beautiful," said Lucy.

Vanessa smiled. She'd felt a few butterflies as she put on the dress. She'd had a few months to think about Betty had said. Betty was right even though Vanessa had wondered if this was what she really wanted. When she looked into John's eyes as he gave her the roses, she still had that feeling that they'd known each other all their lives. Any doubts seemed to melt away. It didn't make sense, but it felt so right. Looking at the dress, the roses, the babysitter and the jewelry she knew what it all meant. And now, she was excited about what the future held. She headed down the stairs, and everyone stopped talking when she entered the room.

"You look beautiful," said John. "Are you ready to go?"

"Yes," she said.

"Lucy, Stephen and I will have a wonderful time," said Betty. "Don't worry about anything."

John walked her to car.

"I thought it might be a little difficult to get into a truck with that dress so I rented this for the evening instead," he said.

"It's nice. I've always wanted one of these."

"I asked Betty's suggestion for an elegant restaurant, and she made reservations for us there. I don't always do fancy restaurants, but you and I haven't even had our first date yet so I wanted it to be something special."

Vanessa laughed.

"I hadn't thought about it. We haven't had a date, and our kids and Betty already have us married off."

"True," he said.

"I can honestly say that I've never had a date like this one before – ever. I think I'll always remember tonight."

John and Vanessa arrived at the restaurant, where they had a secluded table for two waiting.

"I've driven by this place before, but I've never been inside. Did Betty give suggestions on what to eat here?" she asked.

"She said the prime rib was amazing, and the lobster was 'divine.' That was her exact word."

Vanessa laughed.

"It's nice to see you laugh," he said. "Since I've met you, I've seen a lot of tears."

"Yes, that's true, but I'm hoping my tears are behind me for a while. Things are changing too rapidly to sit back and cry. There's much to do."

"If it's at all in my power, I will do everything I can to make you happy."

Her eyes began to fill with tears.

"Don't make me cry. I don't think this mascara is waterproof," she said, attempting to blot the tears before they fell and made streaks on her face.

"I've been thinking about this since the last time I was here. I wondered how to do this, and I just can't wait until after dessert. That seems to be how they do it in the movies," he said reaching into his jacket pocket.

Vanessa felt her heart jump out of her chest.

He got out of his chair in the restaurant and got down on one knee.

"Vanessa, you have changed my world in the few months I've known you. I feel young again. I never thought I could feel love again, but I do. I love seeing you smile and laugh, and I will do everything I can to put a smile on your face and bring you happiness. Will you marry me?" he asked as the entire restaurant looked on.

Vanessa couldn't stop the tears this time.

"Yes, yes, I will," she said.

Several people in the restaurant began to applaud.

He slipped the ruby and diamond ring onto her finger. It fit.

"This ring belonged to my grandmother," he said as he got back into his chair. "It was meant for the woman I married, but I didn't know it existed until after my parents had died. They didn't approve of my first choice, but I think they'd approve of you."

"Oh how sweet of you to say that. This is the most amazingly beautiful ring I've ever seen, and it fits. I love rubies. They are my birthstone."

"I didn't put that together when I was thinking about giving you this ring," he said.

"It's perfect."

"What type of wedding would you like to have? I don't want to rush things, but I don't want them to drag out either."

"Well, neither of us has any family left. I have a few close friends, and I think Betty should be there," she said.

"Yes, I think she should be too. We could have it here if you'd like."

"This is home for me. I do have some friends here I would like to include," she said. "In a way, I feel badly about selling my parents' house. The developer has put in writing to devote some of the property to a perpetual green space and name it after my family, and I like the idea. I don't want to destroy all of the natural beauty."

"Whatever you want. It's your day, and it's all about you."

"I still have some things I need to take care of back in Nashville. I still have a home there. My house is on the market, and furniture in storage. I hope it sells soon."

"It'll be fine. I don't know when you'd like to do this. Stephen and I feel we are supposed to make a trip to Peru this summer. And I think that it should just be him and me. He has only known me. He never knew his parents, and I've been both mother and father as well as being his grandfather. I'm sure he's a little concerned about having his world turned upside down. Through this trip, I can let him know how important he is to me, and that nothing will take his place."

"I understand that," she said. "Lucy is very flexible, and she hasn't stopped asking when we are going to get married since the moment it entered her mind. She doesn't like it here, and I think a fresh start somewhere else would be good for her."

"So you don't mind moving to Georgia? My home has been in my family for generations. I'd like to keep it that way," he said.

She nodded. They'd talked about it several times before so it wasn't a new idea.

"I think Lucy and I both need a fresh start in a brand new place as I've gone through my mother's things, there's been more pain than joy."

"I guess the only other thing we need to figure out is when."

"The fall here is absolutely gorgeous, and it would be the perfect time of year for a wedding," she said. "The temperature won't be too hot."

John nodded.

While Vanessa and John made plans, Lemachor began to knit his forces with Bandion's army. Bandion had been assigned to Vanessa's family for generations. This was not something either Lemachor or Bandion wanted to do. There had been bad blood between the two of them for many years.

"It seems we have a similar story," Lemachor said to his longtime enemy. "What worked for generations is unraveling before our eyes."

"I don't see any losses at this point. There have only been temporary minor setbacks the worst of which is having to work with you."

"The feeling is mutual, but we have to work together to try and defeat them."

"Try? We will defeat them."

"You know we are no match for Elyon's people once they get into position and begin using the weapons Elyon has given them," Lemachor said.

"We are no match for Elyon, but I don't see him down here, do you? I've seen outbreaks like this over the centuries. They begin having a few what they term as victories over us. It's just us letting them think that. We rise up, and they crumble. It's the same thing over again. It's actually quite boring," Bandion snarled.

"You haven't noticed anything different?"

"That grandfather seems to have a little knowledge, but he's like all the rest of them – weak. He may have won some battles, but he hasn't seen what we are capable of yet."

"True, but you do know, the ancient prophecies say we will ultimately be defeated," Lemachor said.

"I've been waiting for centuries, and it's never going to happen. We keep getting stronger. Why should I be concerned with humans? We've crushed many over the centuries. One child and his doddering old grandfather are of no concern to me. You are stupid for thinking they could actually defeat us. And the females. Please, don't make me laugh."

"I'm not as concerned with the two of them as I am with the Enkeli, who have been assigned to fight for them. Belshazzon was sent to guard the boy."

"Yes, I've seen him. He's never scared me," said Bandion.

"Don't underestimate Belshazzon. There are others at his level. I've found myself at the ends of their swords on numerous occasions. The end is never pleasant. I don't want to encounter them again," said Lemachor.

"You are weak. No wonder they've been gaining ground against you. If Gravinder knew what he was doing, he would have encased you in ice centuries ago. These humans are no match for us. Why haven't you learned that? Very few have remotely come close to tapping into the power Elyon has given them. Maybe they actually could do some damage to us if they figured things out, but I have no worries they ever will. And Elyon is far away in his Jeweled City doing nothing to help them figure it all out."

"Your arrogance should have been your undoing a long time ago. How quickly you have forgotten. You know they have greater power than we do. You've been spreading your lies to them for so long you are starting to believe them."

"You are beginning to bore me," Bandion said and vanished.

15

Vanessa went forward with plans for the sale of her parents' home. She asked to stay in the home until the fall to give her time to sort through her parents' belongings. She often spent time in the inner room where her mother kept the paintings. There was something tranquil about the place, something she couldn't describe. She still couldn't understand why her mother never told her things until one day she discovered several diaries like the ones she'd heard John talk about. In them, her mother wrote about the inspiration for her paintings, her visits to the Jeweled City and her father's insistence that she never tell anyone because he didn't want to be embarrassed by her "crazy" ideas and "silly" talk.

Vanessa wept as she read the descriptions her mother had written of her father. There was a side of him she had never seen. He was never an emotional person. He was a workaholic who was rarely home on nights and weekends. He had several businesses in town, served on numerous boards, and did a lot of charitable work. When he was around, he was always too tired to interact with her. The journals told of how her mother retreated into the secret room to paint what she'd seen and of her relationship with Betty, who was the only person she could confide in.

Vanessa began spending more time with Betty; she was curious about this gift Betty said she had. The two of them usually met for coffee before Betty had to greet the lunch crowd at her restaurant.

"So are you a psychic or a fortune teller?" Vanessa asked Betty on one visit.

"Heavens, no," said Betty. "I just know things sometimes. It's not anything I can control. At first, I thought it was what they call women's intuition, but it was more than that. A picture would flash in front of my mind, and then it would happen. I would think it was odd. It kept happening. Sometimes, I'd know something about a person, and later, I'd find out it was true. Finally, I just got to the point where I told it like it was. I've had people come out and say I was crazy. Some people would first tell me that I was wrong, and then later, they'd come back and apologize. It seems like every time it happens there is a solution to a problem they are facing in the words I tell them, or it gives them comfort and hope that things will be okay."

"Well, we all can use hope, can't we?" said Vanessa as she placed the coffee cups on the kitchen table. She set a pot of hot coffee on the table and sat down.

"Think about it, Vanessa. You've experienced those moments. You knew something about a person, and there was no way you could have. There are times when it's been about a person you didn't even know," Betty said. "It was on the tip of your tongue to say something, but you didn't. "

Vanessa thought for a few moments and then she remembered something from many years before.

"I remember when I was a kid knowing things. My mother was so supportive. She was very excited about it, but then my dad found out. I heard them fighting one night. He told her she was crazy, and he wasn't about to have a crazy daughter who would bring shame and embarrassment to him. She needed to stop filling my head with nonsense. She was crying. I didn't want my mother to hurt so I would shut down those thoughts when they came to me. I ignored them, and after a while, they went away," said Vanessa.

Betty grabbed Vanessa's hands.

"It's okay," Betty said and smiled.

"I believe you when you say that."

As Betty squeezed Vanessa's hands, Vanessa gasped.

"What is it dear?" Betty asked.

"Betty, do you have cancer?"

"I went to the doctor yesterday, and that's what they tell me."

"You keep telling me it's going to be okay. You know what? It is going to be okay. You are going to beat this," Vanessa said.

"Yes, I know. I believe it with all my heart. See, you do know things."

"If you need me at all, please let me know."

"Of course, darlin' I will. They found a tiny lump. I go next week for a lumpectomy. It's all good."

And it was all good, as Betty said. The following week, her doctor performed a lumpectomy, removing a small tumor. There were no other signs of cancerous cells. Her doctor said it was found early and had not spread. She would undergo some radiation treatments, and they thought that would be enough.

John and Stephen visited as often as they could to help Vanessa clear more than 50 years of her parents' belongings. Although the company buying the home had offered to dispose of items, she wanted to make sure there were no other treasures hidden away. They decided on a September wedding near a pond on her family's property.

In between their visits to Tennessee, Stephen and John traveled other places including Dallas, Fargo, N.D., Bozeman, Mont., Omaha, Neb., and Seattle. On each visit, they met with small groups of people who had similar experiences with both Elyon and the Gravine. They started a network to interact with each other and learn more about how to fight. All of this movement on Earth did not go undetected from Gravinder's frozen lair. The sands of his hourglass were barely perceptible. Where there once was a steady stream, there were now only intermittent drops of sand. Time was indeed coming to a close. There would be an epic battle before the end. This awakening of Elyon's army was only a precursor of what would come.

He summoned Bandion and Lemachor.

Bandion's nonchalant attitude disappeared as he groveled before Gravinder's feet. Gravinder had changed his form to be even more frightening than they'd ever seen him. He was taller; his shoulders broader; and his eyes fiercer. He was more than angry.

"Lemachor, you are failing," Gravinder growled. "You know I don't know the meaning of the word 'mercy.' My direct order to you is to destroy John and his grandson by any means necessary. If you fail this final time, you will be placed in the pit. As for you, Bandion, your disdain for your assignment as well as your half-hearted attempt to take out the little one named Lucy has not gone unnoticed. I also am aware of how much you despise Lemachor. You will destroy your two and help Lemachor in the destruction of his two, or you will be placed into the pit forever linked to Lemachor. Do I make myself clear?"

"Extremely, sir," they both said in unison and fled as soon as possible.

The pit was not the place they wanted to be. There were a few that had already been placed there. Constant screams emanated from there. They begged to die as their skins were eaten away only to be replaced and eaten away again. The pain was constant; the torment unending.

"Now do you see?" Lemachor jabbed Bandion. "I was right."

"Who is right is not at issue. Let's make this quick. We need to destroy them, and I'm ready to be rid of you."

One of Gravinder's main problems had always been his underestimation of Elyon and his compassion for this group of humans he'd rescued. It was that immeasurable variable that often ruined Gravinder's plans. As Gravinder gave more troops to help Lemachor and Bandion carry out his plan, so too did Elyon send more Enkeli to assist Belshazzon, and he gave John something he'd been looking for.

John and Stephen had just returned on a long flight from Seattle. They'd had a long layover in Atlanta. Stephen went to bed as soon as they arrived home. For a moment, John thought about heading to the library, but he decided to go to bed too. It wasn't long before he was in a deep sleep, and he began to dream. In the dream, he had stepped out of the shower and headed to the mirror to shave. He wiped the steam off the mirror with a towel. As he looked at his bare chest, he noticed something he'd never seen before. *Was that a mole or a birthmark? What was that?* He glanced down and saw it. It was unmistakable. This birthmark was in the shape of a key.

John woke up and immediately turned on a light. He pulled back his t-shirt, and there it was. It was a birthmark in the shape of a key. Of course, he had seen the mark before, but he never really paid attention to it. Doctors had called it a café au lait spot. He had just thought it was a random pattern until now. John felt he had his answers now. Everything he'd ever needed to fulfill his destiny had always been there with him. The book had always been in the house. The means to understand it had been there. He had a legacy of generations before him who had taught him many things. It all made sense to him now.

He even knew the timing of the Peru trip. He turned and looked at the clock. It was 3 a.m. He headed to the library. It was time to book that trip. He began searching flights for Lima, Peru. He knew their journey would begin there. Where they would go from there he wasn't exactly sure, but he knew they would travel towards the Andes Mountains to meet the people in Stephen's dream. He imagined lots of bus rides as well as some hiking would be involved. He and Stephen had done a fair amount of camping together so he hoped they were prepared, and some hiking. Of course, the climate would be quite different from the one they were accustomed to. There were so many details to consider, but some of them would probably have to wait until they arrived in Peru. He booked the tickets. They would leave in about a month.

John couldn't go back to sleep. He decided to read through some of the journals of his forefathers. He found one from his grandfather that mentioned the day of John's birth.

What a fine young man! It took many years for Jedidiah and Mary to have a child. There was a time we didn't think they'd ever be able to have a child, but after many years, a miracle has come to our family. They have named him John. He seems to be fit and healthy. We have noticed a peculiar discoloration on his chest. Strangely enough, it looks like the key of Elyon. I heard my grandfather talk of others in our family with this particular birthmark, but I had never seen it myself. Surely, Elyon's return is soon. Our young one will see many great things.

John read those words over and over until they were seared into his brain.

When Stephen woke up the next morning, he found his grandfather with his eyes closed and reclined in a chair with the open journal on his chest.

"Hey, good morning," said Stephen.

"Good morning to you."

"What are you doing in here?"

"I booked our trip to Peru. We will leave in about a month."

"Really? That's exciting. Where do we go from the airport?"

"I have no idea," said John, and he chuckled. "We will be winging it. I think we will know more once we are there. We will be traveling and eventually hiking into the Andes. That's what it sounds like from your dream anyway."

"How are we going to do that?"

"We will have to pack lightly. I don't know all of the details, but I do know it will work out. Wherever we've traveled to we've had the right connections with the right people. This will be no different,"

"I saw snow in my dream," Stephen said.

"We will be going in the mountains, and you know it's winter there now. We'll see snow I'm sure. Now that I have everything booked, I need to let Vanessa know."

"Okay," said Stephen.

Vanessa had been preparing breakfast for Lucy. School was out for the summer, and Vanessa was including Lucy in some of the wedding plans. It wasn't going to be a fancy affair, but there were still things to get ready.

"So are you ready to go dress shopping, oh maid of honor of mine," said Vanessa.

"Yes, I want a pink dress," she said.

"Pink is more of a spring color," said Vanessa.

"But pink is the prettiest color of all," she said.

"How about blue? Like a really pretty royal blue," her mom answered.

Lucy thought about it and wrinkled her nose.

"Pink is prettier," she said and shook her head.

"Well, let's see what we can find," said Vanessa.

The phone rang. It was John.

"Hey, we were just talking about going wedding and bridesmaid dress shopping," said Vanessa.

"Ah. That sounds like a lot of fun for the ladies today," he said.

"Yes, it will be."

"I wanted to let you know that we have the Peru trip planned," he said. "We'll leave in about a month. It could be several weeks before we return. Is there anything from my end that I can do to help with the wedding plans?"

"I'll make up a list," said Vanessa. "The invitations have been ordered. The flowers have been ordered. I still haven't decided about the cake. Bless Betty's heart; she really wants to make it and give it to us as a gift."

"Then, let her. It can be her wedding present to us," said John. "If her cakes are anything like her cornbread and fried chicken, then have her make a few cakes and get her to ship some here."

"She's been bringing me samples. They are heavenly," said Vanessa.

"Then, we need a big cake."

Vanessa and John talked for a few more minutes, and it was time for her and Lucy to head to the bridal shop in town. She wanted something simple, but traditional in an off-white and lots of lace. The two of them spent several hours trying on dresses – mainly Lucy because Vanessa found a dress almost immediately. It was everything she dreamed. It was a simple long dress in an eggshell tone with layers of lace and short sleeves. There wasn't a train, and she didn't want a veil. She planned to wear flowers in her hair on that day.

Lucy still insisted on pink despite her mother's best attempts to change her mind. There were several styles of flower girl dresses even though she was not the flower girl. Finally, they chose a dress with a big poofy skirt.

"I look like a cupcake, Mom," said Lucy with a grin. "But I want to be a pink cupcake."

"Are you sure? Pink and red hair don't always go so well together."

"I like pink, and you like pink," said Lucy.

"Fine, we will go with pink."

With the dress chosen, the flowers settled, and Betty making the cake, there weren't too many other details that needed to be worked out. The wedding would overlook a lake. A rental company would take care of chairs and a trellis which the couple would be married under. Vanessa's minister from the church she grew up in would perform the ceremony. Betty's daughter would cater the reception. There would only be about 50 guests. Other plans had fallen into place as well. Vanessa's Nashville condo finally sold, and she'd cleaned out her parents' home enough to where the only items in it were ones she and Lucy needed on a day-to-day basis. Betty had agreed to care for Stephen and Lucy while John and Vanessa went on a weeklong honeymoon in a cabin the mountains.

16

It wasn't long before Stephen and John headed to Atlanta to make their flight into Lima, Peru. Stephen was enjoying all the traveling he had been doing with his grandfather. This would make Stephen's first trip out of the country, and he was excited about it.

"Did you know that the llama and alpaca are related to the camel?" Stephen asked on the plane as he flipped through a book he'd picked up on Peru.

"No, I didn't know that."

"And llamas are bigger."

"You like llamas and alpacas?" John asked.

"Yes, I want to see them."

"Well, we'll find some."

Stephen smiled.

"Cool."

From Lima, they took another plane to Arequipa, and that's as far as John knew where they were going. He'd booked a hotel for one night in Arequipa so they could rest from the plane trip and long layovers in Miami and Lima. They didn't take luggage with them; just a couple of backpacks filled with as much as they could carry. John tried not to show Stephen how nervous he was about this whole thing. He truly felt like he was riding on a wing and prayer. It all seemed crazy to him, but Stephen couldn't know that. Stephen needed to know that John had confidence in him. After much needed rest, John and Stephen headed on their journey on foot. They caught a bus and began their journey toward the Andes Mountains and whatever lay ahead of them.

Bus rides were tiring. After riding on the bus north for several hours, John saw that Stephen needed food. They got off the bus in a small town. He never saw a sign as to where they were. As they stepped off the bus, they looked around for a restaurant. A young man approached them. He looked like many of the Peruvians they'd seen.

"You are John, and you are Stephen," said the man in perfect English.

"Yes, we are," said John, immediately on the defensive. He was disbelieving and distrusting of this person. "How did you know this?"

"I am to be your guide."

"I never hired a guide, and quite frankly, I don't know where we are or where we are going."

The young man smiled broadly.

"This, my friend, is the reason you need a guide. I am Miguel."

Miguel held out his hand to shake John's hand. Warily, John held his hand out.

"Why are you so distrusting? Elyon sent you, and you knew he would make a way for you, didn't you?" Miguel asked.

At the name of Elyon, John dropped his guard. He knew, but he allowed his cynicism to get the best of him. Even though these types of things were beginning to happen on a regular basis, it was still surprising when they did. John smiled and nodded.

Lemachor had followed the duo. There was something familiar about this person named Miguel. Lemachor knew he had to do something.

"Yes, you're right, Miguel," said John.

Stephen's eyes widened. He was amazed at this man who knew them.

"So, Miguel, do you know where we are going? You said you were our guide," John said.

"Of course, I know where I am to take you. Some of the journey we must use llamas to carry your packs into the village. It's up on the mountain and hard to get to. Cars cannot go there as there are no roads."

Stephen smiled.

"Yes," said Stephen. "Llamas. Will I get to ride one?"

"No, you will want to carry your packs on them. There will be a couple ready for us once we need them."

"Can I touch one?"

"Yes, of course, you can."

"You speak English very well," said John.

Miguel just turned and smiled. He did not respond.

"There is a village that needs your help. They retreated into the mountains centuries before as Gravinder's forces caused them to flee from their homes out of fear. They thought if they could get far enough away Gravinder and his evil ones would not be able to find them. But they did. They've been ravaged by disease and fear over the centuries."

John nodded.

"And you, my friend, you have the key," said Miguel, who reached out his hand and pointed at John's chest, where the birthmark was. John thought he probably should have been afraid or at least suspicious of Miguel's knowledge. After all, he'd told no one, not even Stephen about his birthmark. That knowledge broke through the rest of John's defenses. He knew Elyon had sent Miguel and now felt completely at ease. It was almost natural that he knew these things about him and Stephen.

Miguel told them he had a truck that would take them up into the mountains; however, they would have to abandon it to make the final approach into the remote village.

First, Miguel took them to get something to eat.

"How did you know we were coming?" said Stephen.

Miguel just smiled again and did not answer. Stephen didn't quite understand it all. Miguel knew things like Betty did. How was that possible? After their meal, they packed their backpacks into the trucks. Miguel loaded the back of the truck with supplies.

"Do you live in this village where we are headed?" John asked.

"No. I've never been there," said Miguel.

At that, John and Stephen both gave each other a puzzled look. They rode for several hours into the Andes. Some of the mountain roads were treacherous.

"Don't look down."

Lemachor lurked in the background. He thought about pushing the truck over the side, but Belshazzon was there with more Enkeli than he'd seen in a long time. He'd have to bring in some reinforcements. There were several Enkeli with Miguel as well. Several Enkeli at Belshazzon's rank. That scared Lemachor. He wasn't going to give Gravinder that bit of information.

"You don't have to tell me that again," said Stephen. "This is a scary ride."

Finally, they stopped in the middle of nowhere it seemed.

"This, my friend is the end of the road. From here, we walk; however, we have a campsite. We will stay here for the night, and begin again in the morning," Miguel said.

The temperature had dropped significantly. There were sleeping bags and coats in the back of the pickup truck. A tent had been set up for them, and they stayed there for the night.

At daybreak, they found Miguel had already made breakfast for them.

"We will walk for a day," he said. "The llamas are already packed and ready to go."

Stephen pulled out his journal, and he began writing furiously as they ate breakfast. He knew he wouldn't have time to do this again for a while. This was all too fantastic to believe. He wanted to remember it all because he'd never experienced anything like this. Where did those llamas come from? Were they there when they arrived the night before? They weren't near a village at all. John didn't say much. He was trying to divide his logical mind from what was happening. He knew it was real even though his brain screamed out that it made no sense.

"We will get the truck on the way back," said Miguel.

They hiked was long, and the terrain was difficult. The llamas seemed to be faring well on the trek. Stephen liked the animals; they seemed friendly enough even if one of them liked to spit at the other. He thought that was amusing.

The view from their vantage point was amazing. They could see snow-covered mountaintops and valleys. It was cold during this part of their journey. Miguel had provided coats and gloves for them to wear to keep them protected from the elements.

After many hours, Stephen didn't think he could walk any longer. His feet ached, and he was tired.

"Can we sit and rest for a few moments?" Stephen asked.

"Of course," said Miguel.

As they sat down, a man seemed to come from nowhere. He rushed up to them. With jet black hair and a weathered face, he wasn't speaking English, and he was speaking very quickly. John and Stephen couldn't understand what he was saying, but Miguel understood perfectly. Stephen knew this was the man from his dream a few months ago.

All John and Stephen knew was this man was asking for their help. They followed the man for several miles. He led them into a village. They noticed many people in this village. The older man went into an adobe house and motioned for them to follow.

Inside, there were several people including children lying on mats and on beds. All of them seemed to be very ill. They were coughing. A woman went to each person with a wet cloth to wipe their foreheads. They seemed to have fevers; all of them were very uncomfortable.

"All of these people have had this plague," said Miguel.

Stephen looked up. The man was now talking to his grandfather, and John seemed to understand all of the things the man was saying.

"What's going on?" Stephen asked John.

"It seems there was some kind of outbreak of a flu or something. It has killed several people here already, and it has spread very quickly," John replied.

He took off his gloves and told Stephen to do the same.

John touched an elderly and frail woman first. She got up immediately and hugged him. As he bent to touch another one of the sick people, he stopped, and then he looked at Stephen.

"You do it," he said.

Stephen knelt down next to a child on one of the mats. As he touched his hands, his grandfather placed his hands on top of Stephen's. Stephen could feel the warmth from his hands. It seemed to go through John's hands into Stephen's. The child looked to be about three, and he had his eyes closed. Stephen thought his skin was very cold to the touch.

"Keep your hands there," said John as his hands covered Stephen's.

After a few minutes, the boy's skin began to feel warm, and he opened his eyes. His mother picked him up and held him. She was weeping.

One by one, they touched the people, and one by one, they were healed.

Miguel had stepped to the side and watched everything as it transpired.

Once they'd touched all of the sick people, John turned to Miguel as if to ask what they should do next. Miguel just stood there. He shook his head as if to say there was more. John looked at the man who had brought them into the village. He rushed over to John, and he grabbed his hands and kissed them in great gratitude. The man looked up at him and as he did, John noticed a birthmark on the man's cheek. It looked like a small key.

"Elyon?" John asked the man, pointing to the birthmark.

The man touched his cheek. He had already been smiling as he watched his family and friends healed before his eyes. With the mention of Elyon, the man smiled wider, and he nodded several times.

The man spoke.

Miguel replied, "He said he is Nestor, and he thanks you for coming to his village and helping his people. He wants to feed you."

"Thank you, Nestor," said John.

Nestor spoke again.

"He wants you to tell him about Elyon. He wants to know what you know about him," said Miguel.

Nestor led them from one adobe structure into another. John guessed this was Nestor's home. There was an older woman in the home. She was preparing dinner. John knew that Nestor was the leader of this people.

"He wants you to stay a few days," said Miguel. "He said he has many things to ask you."

Over the next few days, John and Stephen shared with them their experiences going through the portal into Elyon's world. He told them about the protective armor, about the Gravine and about the Book of Ancient Wisdom. John was surprised to learn that the people of Nestor's village also had a longstanding history with Elyon. There were things they knew that John did not know. They knew about the key. Many of the villagers had birthmarks similar to his and Nestor's. A few of them, mainly those of a younger generation, had actual keys like Stephen did, but all of them seemed to radiate that light that always showed up wherever Elyon was.

"The key of Elyon is a reminder to you that you are chosen with a purpose and a plan in mind. You were never forgotten," said Miguel. "Sometimes, in this life, it seems there is no meaning or purpose, but there always is. To live without purpose is not to live at all. Nestor wants to know if you have a key, John."

John touched his chest just above his heart.

Nestor smiled and nodded.

"Many have this outward symbol. For others, they have no tangible key, yet they know they are his. It's almost like it's written on the inside of them," Miguel said.

"It's so simple," said John.

"Of course," answered Miguel. "It's all very simple, yet complex at the same time."

"Wait a minute," said Stephen. "I didn't know you found your key. I thought you would have told me. Where is it? I want to see it."

"I'm sorry," said John. "It's almost embarrassing because it's been there all along, and I missed it. It's actually a birthmark on my chest, and it is in the shape of a key. I didn't recognize it. I got so distracted in searching for a key like you had, and it was right there the whole time. I felt stupid."

"I guess I understand. That's actually cool. You have the key on you all the time. I wonder if I have a birthmark somewhere."

"I don't think you do, but that's not what matters," John answered.

Over the next two weeks, Stephen spent a lot of time watching what was going on with his grandfather. There were times when John and Nestor were talking that Stephen could see those fiery creatures he first met in the Jeweled City. He wondered if they were messengers. He noticed that sometimes John wouldn't know the answer to a question Nestor had asked, and then when one of the fiery creatures showed up, words seemed to fill John's mouth.

Stephen also thought he noticed some of the Gravine there.

One night after he'd fallen asleep, he had a dream and in it, he saw lots of Gravine fighting the Enkeli. It was a dream he'd had over and over. They seemed to be fighting over Stephen. Not that that hadn't happened before, but it seemed more intense. He never saw himself in the fight but he often saw John and Belshazzon. He didn't know what to make of the dream. It frightened him a little.

Lemachor wondered what was so earth shattering about this Peru trip. These people were so secluded, and technology hadn't reached them. He thought that they couldn't possibly make an impact.

After two weeks in the mountains, John and Nestor formed a strong friendship. John was curious about Miguel. He never spoke unless it was to translate. Maybe on the return, he could find out more about him.

They left the beasts of burden in the village with Nestor and his people. They didn't need them on their return. They were out of supplies, and the people in the village could use them. With the cold nights, the animals' wool could be used to make blankets and clothing.

The hike back to where they'd parked the truck went much faster than the trip into the mountains. Miguel stayed just ahead of them. There was no time for conversation. Miguel was a man on a mission. His words were few. When he did talk, his words were always related back to the experiences they had on the mountain and the coming battle. They made it back to the truck, and it was still there as they had left it.

"My journey with you has come to an end, my friends," said Miguel as he handed the truck key to John.

"How will you get back to your home?" John asked.

Miguel smiled and gave them his backpack.

John turned away and placed it in the back of the truck.

"We won't leave you here, Miguel," said John.

When he turned back, Miguel was gone.

"Stephen, where did he go?" asked John.

"I have no idea. He was just here," said Stephen. "How does someone disappear like that?"

John opened the truck and looked for some kind of identification for its owner.

He stared at the papers.

"Does it have Miguel's name on there?" Stephen asked.

John showed Stephen the paperwork. It listed John's name and address as the owner of the vehicle. He looked at the gas gauge. It showed the tank was full. He shook his head because that was another impossibility. If the trip had taught the two of them anything, it was there were no impossibilities. They'd seen everything taken care of without logical explanation. John's logic had finally gotten out of the way.

"We have a few days ahead of us to drive," said John. "We might as well get started."

"Six months ago, I would have thought that what just happened was something out of a movie, but it's almost starting to feel like normal," Stephen said.

"Yes, things still surprise me, but in a way, I almost expect things like this to happen."

"It's been some adventure."

"And it's only just begun," said John.

The rest of the journey back to Lima and the airport was uneventful. John was concerned about what he was supposed to do with this vehicle. There were maps in the glove compartment of the truck that they used to find their way back to Lima and the airport. Everything moved like clockwork. John had wondered if they'd be able to make their flight back, but they had plenty of time. As they drove through Lima, John saw a young couple broken down on the side of the road. The man had the hood up on the vehicle as thick black smoke billowed from the engine. It was an older car and had seen its share of wear and tear. A young woman holding a crying baby was next to the car.

John found a place to park and went over to the couple.

"Do you speak English?" John asked.

"Yes. Yes. I do," the man replied.

"Listen, I am returning to America today. I have a vehicle here, and I want to give it to you."

The young man looked stunned.

"I don't have the money to pay you," he replied.

"No, I don't want to sell it to you. I am returning to America, and I can't take this vehicle with me. I just want to give it to you. The only thing I ask is that you take my grandson and me to the airport."

After a few more minutes John was able to convince the young man, who was named Jorge, that he didn't want anything for the truck. They found an office nearby with someone who could notarize the transaction.

Squeezing five people into a truck wasn't going to work so they took Jorge's wife, Isabella, and their son to a nearby park.

"I still can't believe you want to give this to me," Jorge said. "I lost my job not too long ago. It seems everything has gone wrong lately. I've taken small jobs here and there as I could find them. I try to care for Isabella and Gabriel, but I have felt like such a failure. This is the first thing that has happened that has been good for me in a long time. I am so grateful."

"Maybe this is the beginning of good things for you," said John.

He reached into his pocket. He had exchanged some of his American dollars for Peruvian nuevo sol.

"I don't know how much this is, but you take it. It won't be worth the hassle of trying to convert it back to dollars," said John.

"I can't take money from you too." Jorge said.

"You aren't listening. It's probably not much, but I don't have time to convert it back to dollars, and it's certainly not going to help me in the States."

"Thank you," said Jorge as he reached out his hand to shake John's.

John looked down at Jorge's hand. He noticed a birthmark in the shape of a key on his hand.

"Does Elyon mean anything to you?" John asked.

Jorge looked puzzled.

"Elyon? Who is this Elyon?"

"You don't know Elyon?"

"You have a key on your hand," said Stephen.

Jorge looked at his hand.

"It is just a birthmark," Jorge said.

"No, you are part of a scattered group of people," said John. "Do you have an email address? I have to check-in at the airport and get ready for my flight home, but I want to talk with you some more."

"Of course," Jorge said as he wrote it down. "You have been so kind. I want to talk to you again. My wife was overwhelmed with your generous gift."

"Here is my email. There was a reason you and I met. It wasn't by chance."

"Thank you. I will look forward to hearing from you," Jorge said.

Jorge left Stephen and John at the airport.

"There are some coats and camping items in the back of the truck. You can keep them or do whatever you need with them," said John as Jorge started to drive away.

"Papa, why didn't he know Elyon?" Stephen asked after they went through security into the airport and checked in for their flight.

"It's just like Vanessa. Over time, people forget; one generation doesn't tell another. Then you find people like Vanessa and Jorge who are part of this group of people, but they don't realize it. That's the reason I got his email address so I can tell him more. Remember our mission? We are waking up a group of people. Why don't we get something to eat? They take dollars at the airport, and it's a few hours until we leave."

"Yeah, I'm starving. How long before we get home?"

"Our plane will arrive in Atlanta some time tomorrow morning. We fly from here to Miami, and we will be there for several hours," John replied.

"I'm ready to be home for a while."

"Well, you will be home for a few days, but we have a wedding to get ready for. Speaking of wedding, I am going to check in with Vanessa. I should be able to use my cell phone from here."

"Just give me food, and I'll be fine," Stephen said and laughed.

When John turned on his cell phone, he did find a few messages from Vanessa telling him how much she missed him.

"Hey, beautiful one," he said.

"Hi. I've missed you so. Are the weary travelers returning? This was the day you had your return flight scheduled," she said.

"Yes, we are in the airport now. Our flight leaves in a couple of hours. It all worked as though we were on a schedule. We couldn't have planned it any better."

"I'm so glad you called. I can't wait to talk to you."

"Yes. I have so many things to tell you about the trip. We'll need a few days of rest before we can come see you again."

"Not a problem. I think we have things under control here. Everything is planned and confirmed for the wedding. We still have about a month left. I hope there won't be any last minute surprises," she said.

"Glad to hear it."

"I'd love to stay on the phone with you for the next two hours until your plane leaves, but I want to save some of the stories for when I see you again."

"That sounds good to me. I've missed you so much. I'll be glad when we're all traveling together."

"I'll see you soon," she said. "I love you."

"I love you too," he replied and hung up the phone.

17

The next few weeks were a blur for Vanessa and Lucy as the final touches were being put on the nuptials.

"Good morning, Betty, come on in," said Vanessa as she welcomed Betty into the house.

Betty gave Vanessa a motherly kiss on the cheek.

"How are you doing, sweetie?" she asked as she headed toward the kitchen for their morning ritual.

Lucy looked up from her computer. They had already started with the homeschooling for the year. Summer seemed to have flown by quickly.

"Good morning, Miss Betty," said Lucy as she gave her a hug and ran back to the computer.

"I have your coffee ready this morning," Vanessa said. "I am going to miss our morning chats. They've helped me so much over the past couple of months."

"I will miss them too, but life's all about change. We move and grow," said Betty. "Besides, if you are in a bind, you can give me a call any time."

"I can't believe the wedding is almost here. There are still so many loose ends to tie up."

"Well, we've got the food all taken care of."

"That means so much to me. I have to go to the bridal shop tomorrow to pick up my dress."

"And mine too," yelled Lucy from the other room.

"Yes, and yours too."

"My pink dress," said Lucy, emphasizing the color.

"Yes, your pink dress."

Vanessa looked at Betty and winked.

"She's ruining my color scheme," said Vanessa and laughed.

"Pink is always in season," said Betty.

"If you're Lucy, then it is. She thinks everything should be pink."

Vanessa looked into her coffee cup. Her mind was miles away.

"It's two weeks from now. It was only a year ago that I was living in Nashville, had a career and a nice little life for Lucy and me, and everything has changed," said Vanessa. "I'm blown away."

"There've been a lot of good changes," Betty said.

"Yes. I know. So, should we go over our checklist?"

"How many times have you gone over it today already?"

"About a dozen," Vanessa said laughing.

"You can't let your past losses dictate your future. Don't let fear of the unknown rob you of the known."

"You're right. I'm so glad to have you in my life without Mama," Vanessa said and gave Betty a hug.

"I'm glad to be here for you."

The next two weeks flew by as the final preparations were made. Vanessa woke up early that September morning. The leaves hadn't quite started to change yet. Summer stayed longer than anticipated so instead of gold, red, and orange hues, there were many green leaves still on the trees, but it was still a magnificent view where the simple ceremony would take place overlooking the lake. There wasn't a cloud in the blue sky. It couldn't have been more perfect.

Although she'd had her doubts at the beginning about this relationship, Vanessa knew this was what she wanted to do and that it was the right thing to do for her and Lucy.

Across town, John and Stephen got up early and had a hearty breakfast together.

"What's going through your mind today, Stephen?" John asked.

"Everything is going to change," Stephen said. He frowned.

"Not everything. I will always be here for you, and that will never change. You can always count on me."

"Thanks, Papa."

"We'll be gone a week, but I'll only be a phone call away. Try to help out Miss Betty while you stay with her."

"Okay. I like Miss Betty. She tells Lucy and me a lot of fun stories. She's not bad for an older lady."

"I've got a surprise for you. You know there's a pond near Miss Betty's restaurant. We're going to go fishing right after breakfast. We've got a few hours before we have to prepare for the wedding."

"Awesome," said Stephen.

"It'll be our secret. Betty promised not to tell. Vanessa might get stressed over it."

Vanessa checked on the last minute details. The chairs were in place with bows neatly tied to them. There was a rose trellis under which she and John would recite their vows. The florist would be bringing the other flowers later in the morning. There was a tent where the food and cake would be. There really wasn't a lot for Vanessa to be concerned about.

She and Lucy had a special breakfast that morning.

"So can I tell Stephen what to do when I become his aunt? " Lucy asked.

"No, you can't. And you should probably think of him more as an older brother than your step-nephew. This isn't confusing at all, is it?" Vanessa said and laughed. "I guess you're enjoying the idea of having Stephen and John in our lives."

"Yes, but what am I supposed to call John?" asked Lucy.

"I don't know. I hadn't really thought about it. What do you want to call him?" she asked.

"I've got a few ideas. I'll try them out on him," she said.

"Okay. You and I have a busy morning. We have to go into town for our hair appointment. We have to look beautiful for today," Vanessa said.

"Oh all right, but Mama, you look beautiful every day."

"Thanks sweetie. I need to look extra beautiful today."

Vanessa's appointment with Sally at the beauty salon included the full treatment – hair, nail,s and make-up. Sally took Vanessa's red hair and fashioned it into an elegant up-do with cascading ringlet curls and placed miniature white roses in it.

Lucy giggled as Sally curled her hair and showed her how the curls could bounce with Lucy's movements. She put a few tiny pink roses in Lucy's hair to finish it.

With their appointment finished, it was back to the house to dress.

Betty was there to greet them, camera in hand.

"I'm going to take lots of pictures," she said as she snapped away.

She helped Vanessa step into her eggshell-colored lace gown. They put on Lucy's pink dress careful not to mess up her curls. Lucy began to twirl around the room in her pink dress with its full and flouncy skirt.

"You are the most beautiful bride," said Betty. "And you look like an angel, Lucy. Let's get some pictures."

Vanessa's bouquet was a mix of white calla lilies and white roses. A few miniature pink carnations provided a hint of color. Lucy had a small bouquet of miniature pink and white carnations. Vanessa took a deep breath and looked at Lucy.

"Are you ready?" Vanessa asked.

Lucy nodded excitedly.

"Then, let's do this," Vanessa said.

They walked out of the house toward the pond. When Vanessa and Lucy were in place, Betty motioned for the violinist to begin the wedding march.

Lucy went first, and even though she wasn't supposed to be the flower girl, Lucy wanted to throw rose petals down the satin runner that created a makeshift aisle. Vanessa soon followed to where John stood with his best man, Stephen. Vanessa smiled at them. They were both handsome in their black tuxedos.

John and Vanessa had written their vows which they exchanged underneath the rose trellis.

"Vanessa, because of you, I believe in love again. I believe in the possibility of second chances, and I believe in the future," said John. "I know that this relationship was destined to be. I look forward to the rest of our days together. There are many adventures in front of us."

"John, I didn't think I could ever love again. I thought I had had my one chance, and I planned to live with those memories for the rest of my life. With you, I've been able to laugh again, hope again, and live again. I look forward to those adventures with you," she said.

As the minister pronounced them husband and wife, Lucy threw her flowers in the air and screamed "Yes!"

Vanessa and John just laughed.

"She will make your life an adventure," Vanessa said to John.

"That's fine by me."

For the reception, it was Southern-style after church picnic fare, featuring Betty's recipes cooked by her daughter, Bobbie. There was fried chicken, potato salad, collard greens, creamed corn, black-eyed peas, tomatoes, and cornbread. There were several different types of pies, and of course, a traditional tiered wedding cake made by Betty. The reception lingered into the early evening as the sound of the crickets and the frogs by the water began to drown out the gentle strumming of the guitarist hired to play.

Vanessa and John changed out of their wedding attire and headed for their honeymoon. The two were going higher into the mountains to a small cabin while Stephen and Lucy stayed with Betty.

There wasn't any car decorating, rice throwing or bubble blowing for the newlyweds. Most of the guests departed long before the couple did. John was a little nervous at the thought of Stephen staying without him. Since Stephen moved into John's home, he'd never been gone for more than a few hours and never overnight. There was an extra sense of anxiety now, and John couldn't quite figure out why.

Lucy had stayed with her grandmother each summer for several weeks and with her independent spirit, she was only too happy to see her mother go away for a few days.

"I'll be fine, Mama," she declared.

"If you need us, you have our cell numbers, Betty," said Vanessa.

"Yes, yes, go on with the two of you. I've raised my own young'uns and helped raise my grands. We'll all be fine," said Betty as she hugged them both and kissed both John and Vanessa on the cheek

"Stephen, if you need me, or if you have anything happen – like a dream or something, call me," said John.

"I will, Papa," said Stephen. "It will be okay."

"Are you ready?" Vanessa asked John.

He nodded, and they headed off.

Betty stayed at Vanessa's homestead with Lucy and Stephen. The developers would take over the property after John and Vanessa returned from their honeymoon. The house was mostly vacant with just the bare necessities, but Stephen had all of his vital electronics including video games. But the two of them really liked being around Betty because she told the most amazing stories and sometimes, she'd tell them things about the future. Tonight though, Lucy wasn't up for any of that. She collapsed into bed almost immediately after her mom left.

Stephen, on the other hand, was wide awake.

"Miss Betty, what do you see about me?" Stephen asked.

"I don't see what I want to see or know what I want to know. I only know what I know. That's not how the gift works. I'm not a fortuneteller. I can't look into a crystal ball and tell you who you will marry in 15 years or however long it takes. I just know what I know when I know it."

"Then how is it useful?"

"Well, maybe it's not what you want to know, but it's what you need to know. Sometimes, we don't know the things we want, but there are times we need to know something. Does that make sense?" asked Betty.

Stephen nodded slowly, but the scowl on his face made it clear he wasn't 100 percent sure.

"Maybe Vanessa didn't want to hear that she was going to get married again, but she needed to hear it. She told me she already knew it in her heart, but when I told her what I had to tell her, it let her know it was okay for her to want that. She still loved her other husband who had died. Sometimes, people feel like they aren't honoring the memory of the dead by getting married again. Vanessa felt like she was betraying him in some way because she had feelings for someone else," she said.

"I think I understand."

"And sometimes, it's not as complicated as that. A lot of times it just brings a sense of hope to people that when a storm in life comes, they have a knowledge that things are going to get better."

Stephen looked straight into Betty's eyes.

"I know that you know something about me, but you aren't telling me. You were afraid to tell my grandfather, too," he said with a calm sternness that made him appear much more mature than his 12 years. "Miss Betty, I know, and I'm afraid too."

Betty looked down and nodded.

"You're right. I have seen something, but I couldn't tell John," she said. "You're about to go through the toughest challenge of your young life. It will be a defining moment for you, but it'll be painful. You still don't know who you are, and you don't know the power that Elyon has entrusted to you. You don't know how to use your weapons or your armor. This will be a matter of life or death – your life or death. It's coming soon. Elyon has given you everything you need, and you'll win only if you follow what you've learned. I couldn't tell John because he can't be the one to help you this time. There are some lessons you must learn on your own. No one can teach them to you, and no one else can learn them for you."

This didn't seem strange to Stephen. He knew that there were still things for him to learn. He had seen the Gravine lose, but mainly when his grandfather was around. If Stephen was to lead a group of people, he would have to know how to gain mastery over them. Elyon had banished the Gravine. Elyon had given him a sword and a defense; Elyon had given him authority; Elyon also gave him a powerful ally and protector in Belshazzon.

"Why didn't you want to tell me this?" Stephen asked. "You know the time is close."

"I've seen a lot of people who had everything you have and more be totally destroyed by the Gravine," she said. "They didn't listen to me. They didn't heed my words. They thought they were strong enough. They had easy victories in their past. They were lulled into thinking the Gravine were weak. And they thought they could do it without using what Elyon had given them."

Stephen let her words sink in.

"I've known all that you said, but I also know that I can't defeat them on my own. Someone else has always been there to help me. Papa has been so distracted in the past couple of weeks that I haven't been able to talk with him about anything except the wedding," said Stephen. "I've been having dreams. They are all the same. I see multitudes of Gravine, and I feel so alone."

"You aren't alone. Never think you are alone, but know that you'll be defeated if you go against them alone. When Elyon's scattered people awaken to who they are and their purpose, he will return to get them, and he will utterly defeat the Gravine. They'll go to their final punishment. You have been working to get his people ready. And you, Stephen, are a threat to them. I've seen a lot of potential threats eliminated."

"I don't want to be eliminated. I want to do what I promised Elyon I would do. How will I be ready?" he asked with a pleading sound in his voice.

"If you keep that attitude, then you'll do just fine. It's when you get cocky and full of yourself that you can't see. It's been a long day. You should go to bed."

Stephen went upstairs, but Betty stayed awake. She'd seen the Gravine that day. They were everywhere, and she knew Stephen saw

THE KEY OF ELYON

them too. Stephen didn't want to go to sleep. He had a sense of dread especially with Betty's words ringing in his ears, but he'd known for a while that something was coming. He just didn't know how soon her words would be fulfilled.

He drifted off to sleep slowly.

Bandion and Lemachor had been waiting. They had gathered reinforcements and were planning their attack outside the home.

"The old woman almost ruined this moment for us," said Bandion. "We strike now. The grandfather is out of the way."

Bandion pointed to several Gravine.

"You, you, and you take out Belshazzon. He's strong, but if you work together, you can weaken him."

Bandion looked around.

"You, you, and you take out the old woman and her Enkeli handler," he said. "She has some strength too, but neutralize her and keep her away from the boy. Do not let her get to him."

Bandion addressed the others.

"The rest of you be on watch. Belshazzon will call other Enkeli, and they will arrive with lightning swift speed. All you have to do is keep them away from Belshazzon and the boy. Lemachor and I will take him out," Bandion said.

Bandion looked at Lemachor.

"Let's get this over with. I want to rid your stench from my nostrils forever," said Bandion.

Bandion and Lemachor flew from the grassy wedding site toward the house and into Stephen's room. Belshazzon was surrounded by the Gravine. He had both of his blades of light fighting them. They had him occupied. Bandion turned to look out the bedroom window. The lawn was lit up like the afternoon with all of the Enkeli using their blades of light to fight against the Gravine.

Lemachor jumped onto the bed and grabbed Stephen around the throat. He pinned him there. Stephen felt like he was in a dream. He could see his body below him and the creature on top of him, but he couldn't feel anything. He looked down and saw he was completely dressed in his soldier suit. In his hand was a blade of light similar to what he saw the Enkeli using.

"You puny human. You are no match for me. You die tonight. We do not give up so easily," Bandion taunted.

"Elyon," Stephen screamed.

At the mention of Elyon's name, Bandion screamed. A ray of light cut across Bandion's face.

"Elyon," he yelled again. Another ray cut across his chest.

"Lemachor," Bandion growled.

Just then, Lemachor placed one gnarled hand over Stephen's mouth. Stephen could barely get a word out.

Betty was downstairs as the Gravine came toward her. One of them punched her in the chest. She crumpled to the floor. Lucy woke up. She knew something wasn't right. All was quiet in the house, but Lucy could smell something horrible. It was like rotten eggs. She got up to check it out; she peeked outside her door, and she saw three Gravine guarding Stephen's door.

Immediately, she grabbed her cell phone. She frantically tried dialing her mother's number. A voice came across the line.

"All circuits are busy. Try your call again later," it said.

She tried several times but got the same message.

Lucy only had a few numbers programmed into the phone because it was only for emergency. John's number was there as well.

"All circuits are busy. Try your call again later," it said.

Lucy started to become afraid. She looked in the corner of her room. She had seen the Enkeli when she went to the Jeweled City, and there was a man in her room who looked like one of them. He had red hair like hers, and she could see freckles. Then she remembered. She saw him the time she was in the hospital.

He put his finger over his mouth to indicate she should be quiet. "Don't be afraid," he whispered.

Lucy continued to frantically dial the phone.

"Come with me," he said. He wore a long cape, which he stretched out as if to shield her. They walked out of the room unseen by the Gravine at Stephen's door.

John woke up. He jumped out of bed to check his phone.

"What's the matter?" Vanessa asked.

No missed calls; no texts and no voicemail, but John just couldn't shake that there was something amiss.

"Everything is fine. Betty will call if there is something wrong," Vanessa said.

Although not reassured, John tried to go back to sleep.

The Enkeli led Lucy down the stairs to Betty who was lying on the floor. The Gravine left her there.

"Are you okay?" Lucy asked as she shook Betty.

Lucy tried not to be too loud. She didn't know what was going on, and she didn't want anyone or anything to hear her.

"Miss Betty," she leaned over and whispered in her ear. "Miss Betty."

"Call an ambulance, Lucy. Do you know how to do that?" Betty answered weakly.

Lucy called 911. An ambulance arrived shortly, but the paramedics couldn't see everything that was taking place in the house. They checked on Betty. She claimed she was fine, and simply passed out from the excitement of the day.

"Please check on Stephen," she told one of the paramedics. "He's upstairs."

Lucy had also called Bobbie, and she arrived seconds after the paramedics did.

"Bobbie, I'm going to be fine," said Betty. "This isn't about me. It's about Stephen."

Bobbie ran upstairs and into Stephen's room.

"Come quick. There's something wrong," said Bobbie as she ran back down the stairs.

The paramedics ran upstairs. One of them leaned toward Stephen's mouth where Lemachor's hand was covering it.

"He's not breathing," the paramedic said. He tried to feel for a pulse in Stephen's neck, where Lemachor's other hand was choking him.

"There's no pulse," the paramedic barked.

They pulled out the defibrillator.

"Clear," he yelled as they attempted to bring back his heartbeat.

The paramedics were unaware of the tremendous amount of warfare going on around them as Belshazzon struggled against the three Gravine. Several additional Enkeli had come to Belshazzon's aid, but immediately, they were swarmed with more Gravine. The piercing of the blades of light seemed to do nothing to the Gravine. As one was injured immediately another took his place.

Stephen looked around and then he looked down. It was strange because he could see what looked like his body with the paramedics working on him. He turned to see Belshazzon. He didn't understand what was going on. In his hands was a sword. It had an ornate handle, but its blade resembled that of the swords he saw the Enkeli use. He knew what he had to do. He took his light blade and ran it through Lemachor who released his grasp from Stephen for a few moments. Stephen could hear the paramedics talking.

"Okay. I have a heartbeat. There is faint breathing. Let's go; let's go," said the paramedic as they rushed Stephen downstairs and out of the house.

Bobbie stayed by Betty's side.

"Another ambulance is on the way," said Bobbie.

"It's not me they're after. It's Stephen. They just had to get me out of their way," said Betty.

Bobbie looked at Lucy. Her eyes were wide, and she looked on the verge of tears.

"It's okay, baby," said Bobbie as she grabbed the terrified child, placed her in her lap and hugged her.

"What's wrong with Stephen?" Lucy asked. "I saw these awful, horrible looking monster things like the ones I saw when I went to the hospital. They have Stephen now. Are they going to kill him?"

"It's okay. Stephen's going to be just fine," Bobbie kept saying over and over, gently rocking Lucy and holding her mother's hand at the same time.

"Bobbie, someone has got to get John or Vanessa on the phone," said Betty.

"I can't. I've been trying. My phone doesn't work. It keeps saying there is no signal and to try again later," said Lucy. She started to cry not because she was sad but because she was so angry that she couldn't do anything to save Stephen.

The other ambulance arrived, and everyone was headed toward the hospital. Bobbie followed behind them with Lucy in the car. Betty ended up in the emergency room not far from where Stephen was.

"I'm the guardian for the little boy. I have the power of attorney while his grandfather is on his honeymoon," she told the doctors. "We haven't been able to get through to him yet."

As doctors tried to bring Stephen back to consciousness, Stephen was fighting against Bandion and Lemachor in their realm. He could still see Belshazzon and the others furiously brandishing their blades.

Stephen's mind was racing.

What else was in the book? he thought. *Nothing seems to be working. Why?*

Little did Stephen realize, but there were others watching him including Elyon.

"Do you want us to go to him, sir?" an Enkeli even taller and broader than Belshazzon asked Elyon. He had several more Enkeli flanking him.

"Not yet. He's like the butterfly coming out of the cocoon," said Elyon. "He is gaining knowledge he must have for the future. He will come out of this stronger and bolder. I will not abandon him to fail."

John woke up again. This time he wasn't going back to sleep. He saw someone who resembled Miguel. John blinked a few times. It couldn't be real. Miguel nodded at him as though he read John's mind. As he got out of bed, Vanessa woke up.

"What's wrong, John?" she asked sleepily.

"I'm sorry. I've got to go. Something is wrong. I don't know what it is, but I know," said John as he quickly dressed.

"You aren't leaving me here," said Vanessa.

"Then, you'd better hurry," he said.

Within five minutes, they were in the car for the two-hour ride.

Bobbie stood outside the doors of the emergency room entrance with Lucy desperately hitting redial.

"It's ringing," Bobbie told Lucy.

"Hello," said John.

"John, this is Bobbie. It's Stephen," she said.

"Yes, I know. We are on the way, but it will take us about two hours to get there. Exactly what is going on?"

"I'm not getting much. Mama passed out, and she told the paramedics to check Stephen while they were there. He wasn't breathing, and he didn't have a pulse. I don't know much else. I'm not his family so they won't tell me anything, and Mama is in a bed in the ER while they check her out. Lucy is with me, but she's shaken. This is the first time we've been able to get through to you. We have been trying for about three hours to reach you, but the circuits have been busy. I'll give your number to the doctors right away."

Vanessa saw tears coming out of John's eyes.

"We'll be there as soon as possible," he said and put his phone down.

"What's going on?"

"I knew something was going to happen. I knew it. I can't lose him. I just can't lose him. He means more to me than life itself."

"John. What?"

"They're trying to take him out. I lost my son. I can't lose my grandson. He's in the hospital. They don't know what's going on," said John as tears began to stream down his face.

The one thing John had feared. He'd worked so hard to protect Stephen. He kept him insulated from the world, but it was happening anyway. He couldn't lose this child too.

John cleared his throat and tried to talk.

"Betty had a heart attack, but the Gravine are trying to kill my son," he whispered.

Vanessa noticed John didn't call him grandson this time. It was son instead.

"He had no pulse; he wasn't breathing," he said.

"You can go and touch him, and he will be fine."

"It may not be that simple. There's a reason they waited until I was out of the way before they struck him."

"Do you want me to drive? There's no reason we should end up in the ER as well. Driving faster on these winding roads is not going to help us get there quicker."

"I'm sorry. I should've left the first time I woke up," he said.

Bobbie told Lucy to stay in the waiting room.

"I'll be right back," she said.

She walked into Betty's room.

"I got John on the phone. They were already on the way home," said Bobbie.

Betty smiled weakly and looked at the nurse.

"Can I go and see him?" she asked.

"Ma'am, I don't know that that is a good idea," the nurse replied.

"Please, I am fine. I promise. You can tell that."

"I'll go ask your doctor," she said and left the room.

Instead of the nurse returning, Dr. Ed Brown, Betty's primary care physician and longtime friend, came into the room.

"Betty, you gave me a scare," said Dr. Brown.

"I am fine. Let me see the boy," she said.

"You can go in there, but they have him hooked up to a lot of machines. Be prepared for what you see. I'll let you go in for now, but you are staying here through tomorrow. Do you understand me?"

"Yes, I understand you. I'm supposed to be caring for that boy. I have to know how he's doing."

"Let's get you into a wheelchair first," he said. "They've moved him to ICU."

"Could I bring Lucy in?" Bobbie asked.

"It's irregular, but I'll go in with Lucy and Betty. Bobbie, you'll have to wait outside," Dr. Brown said.

Bobbie nodded as Dr. Brown pushed Betty down the hall and into an elevator. From there, he pushed her into Stephen's room. He was hooked up to multiple monitors. One of the doctors was reading a chart when they came in.

"Dr. Snow, this is Betty Alford, she is the child's interim guardian while his father is away," said Dr. Brown.

"I understand this has been a rough night," Dr. Snow said.

"Yes, everything was fine, and then I passed out. He seemed to be fine when he went to bed. He wasn't complaining of any aches or pains or sickness," she said.

"Why did you send the paramedics to see about him?" Dr. Snow asked.

"Women's intuition, I guess. He's all I could think about as I was lying on the floor."

"We are doing some blood tests. Nothing has come back yet. His breathing stopped, and his heart had stopped. We don't know for how long. We don't know if there is any permanent damage. His heart rate is fine now. In fact, all of his vital signs are normal. I don't understand what happened. He doesn't appear to have had a seizure. We are looking at all of the possibilities," said Dr. Snow. "Is his father on the way?"

"Actually, it's his grandfather, but John is Stephen's guardian. He just got married again yesterday. They were on their honeymoon. My daughter reached him not long ago. He is about an hour away now I guess."

Stephen tried to hear what they were saying, but it was difficult. His body was in the one world, but yet, he was fighting in the world of Elyon and the Gravine. He felt himself getting stronger. He heard the words of Elyon and the words he had read in the book. They echoed through his mind. Each time he spoke words from the book or said the name of Elyon, he gained ground on Bandion and Lemachor, but they wouldn't completely back down. The two were strong, and as they fought, they brought others in to fight alongside them. They seemed to be fighting for their lives as much as Stephen was fighting for his.

As Stephen fought, he had no sense of time nor of being tired. Their swords had not penetrated his gear; however, he could see the marks upon their bodies.

John pulled up to the emergency entrance of the hospital and got out of his truck without even turning off the engine. Vanessa slid to the driver's side and took over. She had never seen him this upset. He was always calm and collected. This was very disturbing to her. John ran into the emergency room.

"My son. I need to find my son," a shaken John said to the nurse.

"You are the father of the 12 year-old?" the nurse said.

"Yes, yes, where is he?" he asked.

"I need your insurance information," she told him.

John reached into his pocket and handed her his wallet.

"Just take whatever you need out of there and take me to my son," he said.

"They've moved him to intensive care. I'll need some information," she said.

"Please just take me to my son. My wife is parking the car. Can't she give you the information when she comes in?" he pleaded.

As they were talking, Bobbie spotted John. She'd walked back downstairs to wait for them.

"They've taken him to the ICU. Mama and her doctor just went up to see him," she said.

"Please someone take me to see him," John said.

He looked as though he was going to cry.

Vanessa parked the car and came into the ER.

"Vanessa, please fill out paperwork so I can go to see my son," said John.

"ICU is on the fourth floor and to the left of the elevators," the nurse said.

He quickly headed to find Stephen.

When he arrived, he could see Betty, Lucy, and Dr. Brown heading out of the ICU.

"Where is Stephen?" he asked them.

"I'll take you to him," said Dr. Brown. "But I do want to warn you; he is on several machines. Don't be alarmed when you see him. You will need to put on a hospital gown and mask for his protection as well as yours."

He quickly did as he was asked.

For a fleeting second, Bandion and Lemachor paused and looked at one another. If they could destroy the boy, they could destroy his grandfather without ever laying a finger on him. They had found his weakness. John walked over to the bed, and he placed his hands on Stephen. They felt hot like they always did when someone needed healing, but nothing happened when he touched Stephen. His eyes stayed shut; he did not move, not even a twitch.

Suddenly, Stephen felt electricity surge through his body. He looked below him and saw his grandfather standing over the hospital bed touching his body. The power jolt enabled him to fight all the more. He felt stronger and more invigorated than before. The marks upon the bodies of Lemachor and Bandion were even more evident. His light blade cut through two other Gravine which had joined the battle. Their screams filled the atmosphere as they left the battle.

"I'm going to get Dr. Snow and put Betty in a room. Despite her protests to the contrary, she will be staying here tonight. I'm going to run some tests," said Dr. Brown.

"I'm fine, Dr. Brown. Go find Dr. Snow," said Betty.

"Fiesty as ever, Betty?"

"How long have you known me, Ed? I remember babysitting you when you were still in diapers," she countered.

"Yes, ma'am."

John pulled a chair over to Stephen's bed and placed his hands upon his arm.

"John, it's the Gravine," said Betty.

"Yes, I know," said John. "Betty, I don't blame you. This has nothing to do with you. It's not your fault."

"I should've told you before you left, but I wanted you and

Vanessa to enjoy yourselves together. They want to destroy him, but they won't."

John didn't answer; he just kept looking at Stephen.

"Also, John , you can't do it for him. He has to do this. You can help him, but it's on his shoulders," she said.

John nodded, but he wasn't paying attention to her.

Just then Dr. Snow and Dr. Brown came in.

John didn't look at them, but intently kept his eyes on Stephen.

"We don't know what's going on. We are looking at all of the possibilities from every angle," said Dr. Snow.

John turned.

"Just do what you need to do," he said. "I'll be here."

John stayed right by Stephen's bedside for the next three days. He rarely moved except when doctors or nurses told him to. He refused to eat, but he did drink water. He kept his hands on Stephen's arm. Stephen knew whenever his grandfather left. It was like he had been removed from a power source. Lemachor and Bandion continued their fight without weakening.

As the days progressed, Vanessa became increasingly worried about John. He wouldn't talk to her; he wouldn't eat. When Dr. Snow learned John was not eating, he threatened to put him on IV fluids. John wouldn't listen. He remained at Stephen's bedside. Betty had been released from the hospital the day after she was admitted. All of her tests came back fine. Doctors couldn't find any reason for her to pass out. She kept vigil at the hospital with Vanessa, taking Lucy home as needed.

John kept his mind focused on what Elyon had told him that day when he traveled to the Jeweled City. Elyon told him the best was ahead of him. That meant Stephen could not die. He would keep his hands on Stephen's arm as long as it took.

After a week, Vanessa decided she had to do something.

"John, please eat something. Please rest," she said as she tried to push a tray of hospital food in front of him.

"Vanessa, I have to stay here, right next to Stephen," he said. "I'm fine."

"This is not healthy for you. Sleeping while sitting in a chair with your head on your grandson's bed is not good for you. You have got to leave this hospital room," she said. "John, please. I love you. I can't see you like this. This isn't good for Stephen either."

"No. I'm not going to leave him," he said.

"Just eat then? Please."

"I love you, but I can't leave him. You don't understand."

Vanessa left the room in tears, and as soon as she walked out, John slumped over the bed and slid to the floor. Immediately, Stephen felt the power leave, and he looked to see his weakened grandfather lying on the floor. A range of emotions flooded him. He felt the great love that his grandfather had for him, and Stephen realized how much he loved his grandfather. He was angry at the Gravine for what they were doing to his grandfather and his new family. He was angry because they'd hurt Lucy and Betty. His heart filled with compassion for them and what they must be going through, watching Stephen's still body and watching his grandfather wasting away.

"You've messed with the wrong person," Stephen said as he looked directly at Bandion and Lemachor.

All of a sudden, the fight shifted. It wasn't about what they were doing to Stephen any longer; it was about the other people in Stephen's life who were hurting. The compassion for them was great.

Love, thought Stephen. *That's the key. It was so simple.*

Stephen's armor began to pour out even more light. The Gravine became blinded by it. They began to scream.

At that moment, Elyon looked at the Enkeli who had been awaiting his command.

"He truly knows what the key is now," Elyon said and smiled. "Go and rescue him. He has the heart of compassion for others. Now, he will be able to fulfill his mission. He has won this battle."

With swiftness, the battalion of Enkeli swooped down to the Gravine and Enkeli battlefield. The reinforcements took their blades of light and thrust them into the Gravine. They fell to the ground with tortured cries. Stephen looked at Belshazzon who nodded at him. Stephen addressed Bandion and Lemachor.

"Elyon defeated you, and Elyon commanded you to leave us alone. I take the authority that's been given to me as one of Elyon's subjects, and I state that you have no power here in my life or the lives of these people I love. You have no right to do this any longer. You must go," Stephen said.

He charged at them with his light sword, and Belshazzon followed him. There was a hint of fear in Lemachor's face, but Bandion refused to show any weakness. It didn't take long before Stephen had pierced through Lemachor's flesh, and Belshazzon had punished Bandion. Bandion and Lemachor fell to the ground. They knew they were defeated. Now it was time for Gravinder's punishment.

Stephen sat up in the bed and pressed the nurse call button.

"Papa," he called out to his grandfather.

He tried to get out of bed, but there were IVs and monitors and too much equipment. As he moved around, he began setting off all kinds of alarms. It didn't take long for a team of nurses to descend upon Stephen's room. They picked up John from the floor.

"Papa, I'm fine. Go eat," he said.

Vanessa had lingered in the hall after exiting Stephen's room and saw all of the nurses head inside. She followed.

"Are you okay, sir?" they asked.

"I'm fine," he said and saw Stephen.

"Please, let me hug my son," he said.

John pulled Stephen close and tried to hold back the tears.

"I was so afraid of losing you."

"I love you, Papa," said Stephen.

"I love you, son," he said.

"Sir, we need to check him," said one of the nurses.

John nodded and moved out of the way.

He hugged Vanessa.

"I'm sorry. I had to be there for him," he said.

"I understand that, but you have to take care of yourself," she said.

"I'll take that food now."

The doctors were stumped. They couldn't explain what had happened to Stephen or how he pulled out of it so quickly.

Stephen asked for a hamburger and French fries.

Dr. Snow pulled John aside.

"This is the strangest thing I've ever seen. None of our tests show that anything ever happened to this child, but he was in a coma for several days. According to the paramedics, he was dead when they arrived on the scene. I can't explain this. I've run every test I know, and there's nothing wrong. What's even more bizarre is that there are no signs that anything has ever been wrong. There should be something," he said. "I am going to keep him for observation for another day."

"That's fine," John said.

"And how are you?" Dr. Snow asked. "Do I need to check you out?"

"No, I'm just fine now that my son is okay," he said.

"I thought he was your grandson," Dr. Snow said.

"Technically, he is," John choked up. "But he's my son."

"One more night, and if it all checks out, then you are free to go," Dr. Snow said and then he stopped and looked at Vanessa.

"Now, I remember you. You have a little girl who came in about six months ago. She was in a coma, and then all of a sudden she was fine," he said.

"Yes, that's us," she replied.

"Don't take this the wrong way, but I don't want to see your family again – at least, not under the circumstances we keep finding ourselves."

"Agreed."

They moved Stephen from ICU into a regular room.

That night, Stephen had his hamburger and French fries, and instead of him listening to Betty's stories, Betty listened to his.

"Papa, I know what the key is," he told John. "It's love and compassion. The battle wasn't won until I realized it wasn't about me, but it was about you and Vanessa and Lucy and Miss Betty and all those people we have been sent to. Without love and compassion for them, none of this matters. And nothing is impossible when you love someone.

"You are so right," said John. "You are so right."

In the lower regions of Gravinder's icy lair, Lemachor and Bandion cowered in front of their master.

"There are no words. You have failed, and you know what that means," he said. "Chain them together."

Lemachor and Bandion tried to beg for mercy. In the icy pit, their flesh would be eaten away to nothing then it would reappear only to be eaten away all over again. They had heard the screams of those being devoured daily. They were horrific. Bandion and Lemachor's hatred for each other would compound their suffering. Two Gravine bound them in shackles and then shackled one wrist to the other and one ankle to the other. They threw them into the pit where the torment began.

"Bring me Trackeen," said Gravinder.

Trackeen was another Gravine, but his shape was different from Lemachor's as he was higher ranking. He appeared to be half-man, half-animal. He stood more upright than Lemachor and Bandion. His torso and trunk were the same orange-red as Gravinder. He had bulging upper arm and chest muscles. He had a lower body like that of a bull. He had a set of horns on his head like a rhinoceros and long, sharp vampire-like teeth.

"It's been centuries since you've called for me, master," said Trackeen.

"Trackeen, you have a new assignment," said Gravinder. "A human and his grandson think they've won a major battle. He could be one of those that prophecy has foretold. They're wrong, and I need you to prove it to them."

"Of course," said Trackeen.

"Bandion and Lemachor have failed me for the last time

concerning these two, and they are now in the pit. That's where you'll end up if you fail me."

"Sire, I've never failed you."

"And that's exactly the reason I'm sending you on this. You've destroyed some of the strongest of Elyon's people over the centuries."

"I won't fail you now," he said as he vanished into thin air leaving a puff of orange smoke behind him.

Gravinder walked slowly over to the hourglass.

"You may have won this battle, little boy, but it's far from over," he growled.

If you liked The Key of Elyon, please leave a review at www.amazon.com.

For more of Stephen and Lucy's adventures, read Elyon's Cipher, which is available on Amazon at http://www.amazon.com/dp/B00A6XOBZQ and Elyon's Light: Lucy's Call at http://www.amazon.com/dp/B00D465D6S.

Connect with Charmain Z. Brackett at www.facebook.com/thekeyofelyon and Twitter @CZBrackett.